Winds from Afar

Graphic art
by Bernard Leach

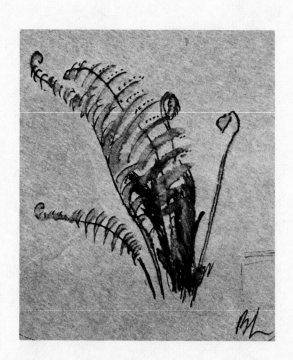

Kenji Miyazawa

WINDS FROM AFAR

Translated by JOHN BESTER

KODANSHA INTERNATIONAL LTD.

TOKYO and PALO ALTO

Distributed in Continental Europe by Boxerbooks, Inc., Zürich; in Canada by Fitzhenry & Whiteside Limited, Ontario; and in the Far East by Japan Publications Trading Co., P.O. Box 5030 Tokyo International, Tokyo. Published by Kodansha International Ltd., 2-12-21, Otowa, Bunkyo-ku, Tokyo 112, Japan and Kodansha International/USA, Ltd., 599 College Avenue, Palo Alto, California 94306 Copyright © 1972 by Kodansha International Ltd. All rights reserved. Printed in Japan.

LCC 72-172216
ISBN 0-87011-171-x
JBC 3094-781222-2301
First edition, 1972

Title page: Brush drawing, Paris.

*Distributed in Continental Europe by Boxerbooks, Inc., Zurich;
in Canada by Fitzhenry & Whiteside Limited, Ontario; and
in the Far East by Japan Publications Trading Co., P.O. Box
5030 Tokyo International, Tokyo. Published by Kodansha
International Ltd., 2-12-21, Otowa, Bunkyo-ku, Tokyo 112,
Japan and Kodansha International/USA, Ltd., 599 College
Avenue, Palo Alto, California 94306. Copyright © 1972, by
Kodansha International Ltd. All rights reserved. Printed in
Japan.*

LCC 75-174216
ISBN 0-87011-171-x
JBC 8093-783222-2361
First edition, 1972

Title page: Brush drawing, *Ferns*

CONTENTS

CONTENTS

FOREWORD

Of the sixteen tales translated here, six have appeared previously in a small volume entitled *Winds and Wildcat Places*. The previous collection was produced essentially as a book for children. In increasing the number of stories and publishing them in the present format, the aim has been not only to create a definitive edition of the best of Miyazawa but also to produce a book that can be enjoyed at least as much by adults as by children.

To do this implies a considerable confidence in the value of Miyazawa's children's stories. To translate works such as these forty years after their author's death and from a language as remote as Japanese suggests that they have acquired a kind of classic status.

Such a status has in fact long since been achieved in Miyazawa's own country. His place in modern Japanese literature is secure. Learned papers are published on him, and new editions continue to appear. His work does not seem to date, for it is read now by a generation quite different from Miyazawa's.

One obvious reason for this is that although his writing is very much a product of the northern country district of Honshu where he lived his short life, his appeal relies basically on qualities unrelated to any particular society or country. The same is true, of course, of most classic children's stories, and in this sense Miyazawa's work easily avoids the barriers that inevitably blunt our response to much in Japanese literature. More important here, though, is the question of what, in the positive sense, Miyazawa offers the adult reader in other countries.

The most obvious elements in Miyazawa's appeal are the charm and inventiveness of his tales. They are all good stories. They have the humor and inconsequentiality, the ability to evoke a world of their own, the absence of theorizing, and the satisfying sense of inevitability that everyone expects of children's stories. With engaging freedom, the choice of characters ranges from wildcats to elderly generals to dustpans. And as most good children's stories do, they comment ruefully on moral questions and the realities that precede and underlie the adult world.

But it is in the way Miyazawa's work, consciously and unconsciously, reflects that world that his special qualities begin to assert themselves. The realm that his characters inhabit is not a cozy middle-class world, but neither do his shapes and shadows harbor barely concealed Freudian horrors. His settings are northern without nordic morbidity. He avoids insipidity without falling into the grotesque. In his cautionary tales he disposes of his villains with satisfying heartlessness, but there is little sadism. Without sentimentality, his world achieves a peculiar sweetness and light.

That Miyazawa was aware of the everyday foibles and stupidities of humanity is clear, of course, from the element of fable in his work. The three episodes of "The Spider, the Slug, and the Raccoon," though humorous, have an unusually sharp element of satire. That he also knew enough of human relationships to have developed a remarkable compassion for their well-meaning blunderings is clear from that moving little tragi-comedy, "Earthgod and the Fox."

Yet still more essential in Miyazawa than this humanism is an intense nostalgia for innocence, for the childlike state that precedes all such things as society and morality. This nostalgia, together with the sensitivity towards nature with which it is so closely linked is, above all, what gives his work its special flavor. The harking back to innocence is not so much a retreat into childhood as a reaffirmation of certain aspects of our relationship with the universe about us. When, as in "The Kenju Wood," this theme of innocence is fairly explicit, it can come close to sentimentality (even though this particular story has a special poignancy in today's polluted world). In other tales, however, it is treated more subtly, while in some—especially in that small masterpiece of economy, "A Stem of Lilies"—it acquires a peculiarly radiant, almost religious intensity.

And here we come close to the heart of Miyazawa's appeal. A similar quickening of the poetic imagination, triggered in most cases by the author's response to nature, occurs sporadically throughout the whole of his work. Basically, it is the strength of his feeling for nature that makes him unique. For Miyazawa, nature is all movement and color. His word-painting, simple though it is, has a freshness of palette, a sense of rediscovery, and an almost unnatural sensitivity that calls to mind some Impressionist pictures. With all this goes a sense of immense space—of distant hills, winds from afar, and infinite depths to the heavens. Not only is his work free of coziness and claustrophobia: he seems positively to go out to meet the loneliness of the universe.

Time and again, this awareness of nature transmutes something quite ordinary into poetry. "The Dahlias and the Crane" would be no more than a charming cautionary tale if it were not also a miniature prose-poem showing the year slipping inexorably from late summer into autumn. "The Fire Stone" might be a routine morality without its recurring images of nature. "Wildcat and the Acorns," superficially one of the more "childlike" of the stories, has a morning freshness that complements the character of the boy Ichiro. And the whole of "The Red Blanket" is a kind of set-piece that magically evokes the passage of a snowstorm from the first uneasy stirrings in the sky, through the height of the blizzard, to the serenity of the sun's return.

Yet this is not quite all. Here and there, in these stories, one is struck by a strength of feeling that borders on ecstasy. It is as though Miyazawa's nostalgia for innocence was accompanied by a longing for complete absorption into the universe, a longing whose intensity is heightened to the point where the only outlet it can find is in ritual. Nowhere is this more clear than at the end of "The First Deer Dance," where the sense of quivering joy goes far beyond what one would expect in a tale that, superficially, is no more than an imaginative reconstruction of the origins of a folk dance. In "The Nighthawk Star," the return to nature finds a different (perhaps slightly more facile) form when the unhappy nighthawk attains release in an almost Christian style apotheosis. In "The Bears of Mt. Nametoko," the hunter forced by circumstances into the destruction of other creatures is finally reconciled with his victims and reabsorbed into the universe in a scene of brooding grandeur that has the mystery of some primeval rite.

But once this element is perceived, it is found recurring, in less obvious ways, again and again throughout the stories. A sunset becomes a ceremony; the bell-flower tolls the indifference of nature to its creatures; the seasons parade past, and man gazes in awe at the solemn procession of the stars. Miyazawa takes us back, not to the nursery but to somewhere freer, more timeless, and more indifferent to ourselves. From time to time, in these seemingly slight, utterly charming tales, he reaches out towards the essence of wonder and the heart of poetry. It is those moments that give them their substance and set the seal on their value for anyone, in any country, who will respond.

John Bester

Tokyo, 1972

9

The Dahlias and the Crane

At the top of a small hill amidst the orchards there grew two yellow dahlias as tall as sunflowers and one dahlia that was taller still, with a great red flower.

The red dahlia was hoping to become queen of the flowers.

When the wind came raging from the south, dashing great raindrops against the trees and flowers and shrieking with laughter as it tore green burrs and even twigs from the small chestnut tree on the hill, the three splendid dahlias would merely sway gently and seem to glow all the more intensely.

And when the mischievous north wind, for the first time that year, went wailing like a flute through the blue sky, the wild pear tree at the foot of the hill waved its branches busily and the fruit fell in the orchard, yet the three tall dahlias merely gave the very slightest of dazzling smiles.

One of the two yellow flowers spoke as though to herself, her attention fixed on the pale blue southern sky near the horizon.

"Today the sun seems to be scattering rather more of his powdered cobalt light."

"You look a little paler than usual today," said the other yellow dahlia, peering earnestly into her friend's face. "I'm sure I'm the same."

"Yes, you are," said the other. "But you," she said to the red dahlia. "Why, how splendid you look today! I feel you might almost burst into flames."

The red dahlia gazed up at the blue sky and, shining in the sunlight, smiled faintly as she replied, "It's not enough. I shan't be happy until the whole sky seems to blaze red with my light. It makes me so frustrated!"

Before long the sun went down, the twilight sky of yellow crystal sank in its turn, the stars came out, and the heavens were a mighty abyss of bluish black.

"Pee-tri-tri," called a crane as it flew by, dark beneath the starlight.

"Crane," said the red dahlia. "I'm very beautiful, aren't I?"

"Very beautiful. So red!"

The bird disappeared into the dark depths of the swamp beyond, calling softly

as it went to a single white dahlia that bloomed there unnoticed, "Good evening."

The white dahlia smiled shyly.

The waxy clouds over the hills turned a muddy white, and day broke.

"Oh!" cried one yellow dahlia in surprise. "How beautiful you've grown—as though surrounded by a pink halo."

"Yes, honestly," said the other, "it's as though you'd gathered around you all the red colors from the rainbow."

"No, really? But I'm bored all the same. I want to turn the whole sky red with my color. The sun's sprinkling rather more gold dust than before."

Both the yellow flowers fell silent and made no reply.

Golden evening gave way to a cool, fresh night of indigo. The feathery crane went flying urgently across the star-studded sky.

"Crane—I shine quite a bit, don't I?"

"Yes, quite a bit."

And as he descended into the dim white mist in the distance, the crane murmured once more to the white dahlia in a quiet voice, "Good evening. How are you this evening?"

The stars revolved, and to Venus's last song the sky turned silver all over and a new day dawned. This morning, the sunlight was all gleaming waves of amber.

"Oh, how beautiful you are! Your halo is five times bigger than yesterday!"

"Really dazzling! Look, your light reaches as far as that pear tree over there."

"Yes, I know. But I hate it even so. Nobody's said that I'm queen yet."

So the yellow dahlias gave each other a sad look, then turned their great eyes towards the hills that rose deep blue to the west.

The fragrant, dazzling autumn day drew to a close; the dew fell and the stars moved round, and the same crane flew silently across the sky.

"Crane—how do I look tonight?"

"Let's see. Why, magnificent. But it's getting quite dark, you know."

And as it passed over the bank of the swamp beyond, the crane said to the white dahlia, "Good evening. A lovely evening."

Day began to break, and in the violet half-light the yellow dahlias glanced over at the red dahlia, then suddenly turned frightened faces towards each other and said not a word.

"Oh, I'm so frustrated," said the red dahlia. "How do I look this morning?"

"Bright red, that's certain. But to us you don't look quite so red as before," said one yellow dahlia.

"How do I look, then? Tell me! How?"

"It's only we who have that impression," said the other yellow dahlia, fidgeting uncomfortably. "Now please don't take it to heart, but it looks to us as though you have dark specks on you."

"Oh, no! Don't go on! You're tempting fate!"

The sun shone all day, and the apples on the hill turned a glossy red on one side.

Twilight descended, dusk drew nearer, and night came.

The crane flew across the sky crying "pee-tri-tri, pee-tri-tri."

"Crane—crane—can you see me tonight?"

"Well, now . . . not very clearly, I'm afraid."

The crane flew on hastily towards the swamp, calling to the white dahlia as it went, "It's a little warm this evening, isn't it?"

A new day began to break.

In the pale white light that smelled of apples, the red dahlia said, "Quick, tell me how I look today. Quick!"

However much the yellow dahlias tried to see the red dahlia, they could only make out something darkish and hazy.

"It's still night, we can't tell."

"No—tell me the truth," said the red dahlia almost tearfully. "Tell me the truth. You're trying to hide something from me, aren't you? Am I dark? Am I dark?"

"Y-yes, it looks like it. But we can't really see properly."

"Oh dear! And I do so hate red with black spots!"

Just then a short man with a yellow, pointed face and a strange, three-cornered hat came along with his hands in his pockets. When he saw the red dahlia, he shouted, "Ah, this one has it! The mark of the Reaper."

And he snapped the stem clean through. The red dahlia was borne off helpless in his hand.

"Where are you going? Oh, where are you going?" cried the yellow dahlias, racked with sobs. "Hold on to us, do! Oh, where are you going?"

Faintly from afar there came the voice of the red dahlia.

The voice grew more distant and more distant still, till finally it was lost in the murmur of the branches of the poplar at the foot of the hill. And the glittering sun rose amidst the tears of the yellow dahlias.

Etching, *Small Oak*

Earthgod and the Fox

On the northern edge of a stretch of open land the ground rose in a slight hillock. The hillock was covered entirely with spike-eared grass, and right in the middle of it stood a single, beautiful female birch tree.

The tree was not actually very big, but its trunk gleamed a glossy black and its branches spread out gracefully. In May its white flowers were like clouds, while in autumn it shed leaves of gold and crimson and many other colors.

All the birds, from birds of passage such as the cuckoo and the shrike right down to the tiny wren, would come to perch in the tree. But if a young hawk or some other large bird was there, the smaller birds would spy him from afar and refuse to go anywhere near.

The tree had two friends. One was the earthgod, who lived in the middle of a marshy hollow about five hundred paces away, and the other was a brown fox, who always appeared from somewhere in the southern part of the plain.

Of the two of them it was the fox, perhaps, that the birch tree preferred. The earthgod, in spite of his imposing name, was too wild, with hair hanging unkempt like a bundle of ragged cotton thread, bloodshot eyes, and clothes that dangled about him like bits of seaweed. He always went barefooted, and his nails were long and black. The fox, on the other hand, was extremely refined and almost never made people angry or offended them.

The only thing was that, if you compared them really carefully, the earthgod was honest, whereas the fox was, perhaps, just a little dishonest.

It was an evening at the beginning of summer. The birch tree was covered all over with soft new leaves, which filled the air about with a delightful fragrance. The Milky Way stretched whitish across the sky, and the stars were twinkling and shaking and switching themselves on and off all over the firmament.

On such a night, then, the fox came to pay the birch tree a visit, bringing

with him a book of poetry. He was wearing a dark blue suit fresh from the tailor's, and his light brown leather shoes squeaked slightly as he walked.

"What a peaceful night!" he said.

"Oh, yes," breathed the birch tree.

"Do you see Scorpio crawling across the sky over there? In ancient China, you know, they used to call the biggest star in the constellation the 'Fire Star.'"

"Would that be the same as Mars?"

"Dear me, no. Not Mars. Mars is a planet. This one is a real star."

"Then what is the difference between a planet and a star?"

"Why, a planet can't shine by itself. In other words, it has to have light from somewhere else before it can be seen. A star is the kind that shines by itself. The sun, now, is a star, of course. It looks big and dazzling to us, but if you saw it from terribly far away, it would only look like a small star, just the same as all the others."

"Well? So the sun is only one of the stars, is it? Then I suppose the sky must have an awful lot of suns—no, stars—oh, silly me, suns—of course?"

The fox smiled magnanimously. "You might put it like that," he said.

"I wonder why some stars are red, and some yellow, and some green?"

The fox smiled magnanimously again and folded his arms gently across his chest. The book of poetry under his arms dangled perilously, but somehow stopped just short of falling.

"Well, you see," he said, "at first all the stars were like big, fluffy clouds. There are still lots of them like that in the sky. There are some in Andromeda, some in Orion, and some in the Greyhounds. Some of them are spiral shaped and some are in rings the shape of fishes' mouths."

"I'd love to see them sometime. Stars the shape of fishes' mouths—how splendid!"

"Oh, they are, I can tell you! I saw them at the observatory."

"Well! I'd love to see them myself."

"I'll show you them. To tell the truth, I've a telescope on order from Germany. It'll be here sometime before next spring, so I'll let you have a look as soon as it comes."

The fox had spoken without thinking, but the very next moment he was saying to himself, "Oh dear, if I haven't gone and told my only friend a fib yet again! But I only said it to please her. I really didn't mean any harm by it. Later on, I'll tell her the whole truth."

with him a book of poetry. He was wearing a dark blue suit fresh from the tailor's, and his light brown leather shoes squeaked slightly as he walked.

"What a peaceful night!" he said.

"Oh, yes!" breathed the birch tree.

"Do you see Scorpio crawling across the sky over there? In ancient China, you know, they used to call the biggest star in the constellation the 'Fire Star.'"

"Would that be the same as Mars?"

"Dear me, no. Not Mars. Mars is a *planet*. This one is a real star."

"Then what is the difference between a planet and a star?"

"Why, a planet can't shine by itself. In other words, it has to have light from somewhere else before it can be seen. A star is the kind that shines by itself. The sun, now, is a star, of course. It looks big and dazzling to us, but if you saw it from terribly far away, it would only look like a small star, just the same as all the others."

"Well! So the sun is only one of the stars, is it? Then I suppose the sky must have an awful lot of suns—no, stars—oh silly me, suns—of course?"

The fox smiled magnanimously. "You might put it like that," he said.

"I wonder why some stars are red, and some yellow, and some green?"

The fox smiled magnanimously again and folded his arms grandly across his chest. The book of poetry under his arms dangled perilously, but somehow stopped just short of falling.

"Well, you see," he said, "at first, all the stars were like big, fluffy clouds. There are still lots of them like that in the sky. There are some in Andromeda, some in Orion, and some in the Greyhounds. Some of them are spiral shaped and some are in rings the shape of fishes' mouths."

"I'd love to see them sometime. Stars the shape of fishes' mouths—how splendid!"

"Oh, they are, I can tell you! I saw them at the observatory."

"Well! I'd love to see them myself!"

"I'll show you them. To tell the truth, I've a telescope on order from Germany. It'll be here sometime before next spring, so I'll let you have a look as soon as it comes."

The fox had spoken without thinking, but the very next moment he was saying to himself, "Oh dear, if I haven't gone and told my only friend a fib yet again! But I only said it to please her, I really didn't mean any harm by it. Later on, I'll tell her the whole truth."

The fox was quiet for a while, occupied with such thoughts, but the birch tree was too delighted to notice.

"I'm so happy!" she said. "You're always *so* kind to me."

"Oh, quite," said the fox rather dejectedly. "Why, I'd do anything for you. Would you care to read this book of poetry, by the way? It's by a man called Heine. It's only a translation, of course, but it's not at all bad."

"Gracious! May I really borrow it?"

"Of course you may. Pray read it at your leisure. Well, I must say goodbye now. Dear me, though—I feel there's something I forgot to say."

"Yes, about the color of the stars."

"Ah, of course! But let's leave that until next time, shall we? I mustn't impose on your hospitality."

"Oh, that doesn't matter."

"Anyway, I'll be coming again soon. Goodbye to you, then. I'll leave the book with you. Goodbye now."

The fox set off briskly homewards. And the birch tree, her leaves rustling in a south wind that sprang up just then, took up the book of verse and turned the pages in the light of the faint glow from the Milky Way and the stars that dotted the sky. The book contained "Lorelei" and many other beautiful poems by Heine, and the birch tree read on and on all through the night. Not until past three, when Taurus was already beginning to climb in the east above the plain, did she begin to drowse ever so slightly.

Dawn broke, and the sun rose in the heavens. The dew glittered on the grass, and the flowers bloomed with all their might. Slowly, slowly from the northeast, bathed in morning sunlight as though he had poured molten copper all over himself, came the earthgod. He walked slowly, quite slowly, with his arms folded soberly across his chest.

Somehow, the birch tree felt rather put out, but even so, she shimmered her bright green leaves in the earthgod's direction as he came, so that her shadow went flutter, flutter where it fell on the grass. The earthgod came up quietly and halted in front of the birch tree.

"Good morning to you, Birch Tree."

"Good morning."

"D'ye know, Birch Tree, there are many, many things I don't understand when I come to think about them. We don't really know very much, do we?"

"Why, what kind of things?"

"Well, there's grass, for instance. Why should it be green, when it comes out of dark brown soil? And then there are the yellow and white flowers. It's beyond me."

"Mightn't it be that the seeds of the grass have green or white inside them already," said the birch tree.

"Yes. Yes, I suppose that's possible," he said. "But even so, it's beyond me. Take the toadstools in autumn, now. They come up directly out of the soil, without any seeds or anything. And they come up in red and yellow and all kinds of colors. It's really beyond me!"

"How would it be if you asked Mr. Fox?" said the birch tree, who was still too infatuated with last night's talk to know any better.

The earthgod's face changed color abruptly, and he clenched his fists.

"What's that? Fox? What's the fox been saying?"

"Oh," said the birch tree in a faltering voice, "he didn't say anything. It was just that I thought he might know."

"And what makes you think a fox could teach a god something, eh?"

By now the birch tree was so frightened that she could only quiver and quiver. The earthgod paced about with his arms folded over his chest, gnashing his teeth loudly all the while. Even the grass shivered with fear wherever his jet-black shadow fell on it.

"That fox is a blight on the face of the earth!" he said. "Not a word of truth in him. Servile, cowardly, and terribly envious into the bargain!"

"It will soon be time for the yearly festival at your shrine, won't it?" said the birch tree, recovering her composure at last.

The earthgod's expression softened slightly.

"That's right," he said. "Today's the third of the month, so there are only six days to go."

But then he thought about it for a while and suddenly he broke out again.

"But human beings are a useless lot! They don't bring a single offering for my festival nowadays. Why—the next one that sets foot on my territory, I'll drag down to the bottom of the mud for his pains!"

He stood there grinding his teeth noisily. The birch tree, highly alarmed at finding that her attempts to soothe him had had just the opposite effect again, was past doing anything except flutter her leaves in the breeze. For a while the earthgod strode about gnashing his teeth, his arms folded high across his chest and his whole body seeming to blaze as the sunlight poured down on him. But

"Well, there's grass, for instance. Why should it be green, when it comes out of dark brown soil? And then there are the yellow and white flowers. It's beyond me."

"Mightn't it be that the seeds of the grass have green or white inside them already?" said the birch tree.

"Yes. Yes, I suppose that's possible," he said. "But even so, it's beyond me. Take the toadstools in autumn, now. They come up directly out of the soil, without any seeds or anything. And they come up in red and yellow and all kinds of colors. It's really beyond me!"

"How would it be if you asked Mr. Fox?" said the birch tree, who was still too infatuated with last night's talk to know any better.

The earthgod's face changed color abruptly, and he clenched his fists.

"What's that? Fox? What's the fox been saying?"

"Oh," said the birch tree in a faltering voice, "he didn't say anything. It was just that I thought he might know."

"And what makes you think a fox could teach a *god* something, eh?"

By now the birch tree was so frightened that she could only quiver and quiver. The earthgod paced about with his arms folded over his chest, gnashing his teeth loudly all the while. Even the grass shivered with fear wherever his jet-black shadow fell on it.

"That fox is a blight on the face of the earth!" he said. "Not a word of truth in him. Servile, cowardly, and terribly envious into the bargain!"

"It will soon be time for the yearly festival at your shrine, won't it?" said the birch tree, recovering her composure at last.

The earthgod's expression softened slightly.

"That's right," he said. "Today's the third of the month, so there are only six days to go."

But then he thought about it for a while and suddenly he broke out again.

"But human beings are a useless lot! They don't bring a single offering for my festival nowadays. Why—the next one that sets foot on my territory, I'll drag down to the bottom of the mud for his pains!"

He stood there grinding his teeth noisily. The birch tree, highly alarmed at finding that her attempts to soothe him had had just the opposite effect again, was past doing anything except flutter her leaves in the breeze. For a while the earthgod strode about gnashing his teeth, his arms folded high across his chest and his whole body seeming to blaze as the sunlight poured down on him. But gradually began to go round and round in circles. At this he grew more and more alarmed, until finally he was going round and round on the same spot, panting desperately all the while. His one idea seemed to be to get out of the hollow as quickly as he could, but for all his struggles he only managed to circle round in the same place. In the end he began to cry nervously and, flinging up his arms, started to run.

This seemed to delight the earthgod. He just grinned and watched without getting up from the ground, until before long the woodcutter, who by now was giddy and exhausted, collapsed in the water. Then the earthgod got slowly to his feet. With long strides he squelched his way to where the woodcutter lay and, picking him up, flung him over onto the grassy ground. The woodcutter landed in the grass with a thud. He groaned once and stirred, but still did not come to.

The earthgod laughed loudly. His laughter rose up into the sky in great, mysterious waves. Reaching the sky, the sound bounced back and down again to the place where the birch tree stood. The birch tree turned suddenly so pale that the sunlight shone green through her leaves, and she began to quiver frantically.

The earthgod tore at his hair with both hands. "It's all because of the fox," he told himself, "that I feel so miserable. Or rather, the birch tree. No—the fox and the birch tree. That's why I suffer so much. If only I didn't mind about the birch tree, I'd mind even less about the fox. I may be nobody much, but I am a god after all, and it's disgraceful that I should have to bother myself about a mere fox. But the awful thing is, I do. Why don't I forget all about the birch tree, then? —Because I can't. How splendid it was this morning when she went pale and trembled! I was wrong to bully a wretched human being just to work off my temper, but it can't be helped. No one can tell what a body'll do when he gets really cross."

So dreadfully sad did he feel that he beat at the air in despair. Another hawk came flying through the sky, but this time the earthgod just watched him go in silence.

From far, far away came the sound of cavalry at their maneuvers, with a crackling of rifle fire like salt being thrown on flames. From the sky, the blue light poured down in waves. It must have done the woodcutter good, for he came to, sat up fearfully, and peered about him. The next moment he was up and running away like an arrow shot from a bow. Off he ran in the direction of Mt. Mitsumori.

22

the more he thought about it, the crosser he seemed to get. In the end he could bear it no longer and with a great howl rushed violently off home to his hollow.

❦

The place where the earthgod lived was a dank and chilly swamp grown all over with moss, clover, stumpy reeds, and here and there a thistle or a dreadfully twisted willow tree. There were soggy places where the water seeped through in reddish, rusty patches. You only had to look at it to feel at once that it was all muddy and somehow frightening.

On a patch like a small island right in the middle of it all stood the earthgod's shrine, which was about six feet high and made of logs.

The earthgod came back to the island. He stretched himself out full length on the ground by the side of his shrine and scratched long and hard at his dark, scraggy legs.

Just then he noticed a bird flying through the sky right above his head, so he sat up straight and shouted "Shoo!" in a loud voice. The bird wobbled in alarm and for a moment seemed about to fall. Then it fled into the distance, gradually losing height as it went, as though its wings were paralyzed.

The earthgod gave a little laugh and was getting to his feet when he happened to glance in the direction of the hillock, not far away, where the birch tree grew. Suddenly he turned pale; his body went as stiff as a poker, and he began to tear at his unkempt hair again, too angry for words.

A solitary woodcutter on his way to work on Mt. Mitsumori was coming up from the south of the hollow, striding along the narrow path that skirted its edge. He seemed to know all about the earthgod, for every now and then he would glance anxiously in the direction of the shrine. But he could not, of course, see the earthgod.

When the earthgod caught sight of the woodcutter, his face flushed with pleasure. He stretched out his right hand in the woodcutter's direction, then grasped the wrist of his right hand with his left hand and made as though to drag it back towards him. And strange to say, the woodcutter, who thought he was still walking along the path, found himself gradually stepping deeper and deeper into the hollow. He quickened his pace in alarm, his face turned pale, his mouth opened, and he began to gasp.

Slowly the earthgod twisted his right wrist. And as he did so, the woodcutter

Watching him, the earthgod gave a great laugh again. Again his laughter soared up to the blue sky and hurtled back down on the birch tree below. Again the birch tree's leaves went pale and she trembled delicately, so delicately that you would scarcely have noticed.

The earthgod walked aimlessly round and round his shrine till finally, when he seemed to feel more settled, he suddenly darted inside.

It was a misty night in August. The earthgod was so terribly lonely and so dreadfully cross that he left his shrine on an impulse and started walking. Almost before he realized it, his feet were taking him in the direction of the birch tree. He couldn't say why, but whenever he thought of the birch tree, his heart seemed to turn over and he felt intolerably sad. Nowadays he was much easier in his mind than before, and he had tried his best not to think about either the fox or the birch tree. But try as he might, they kept coming into his head. Every day he would tell himself over and over again, "You're a god after all—what can a single birch tree mean to you?" But still he felt awfully sad. The memory of the fox, in particular, hurt till it seemed his whole body was on fire.

Wrapped in his own thoughts, the earthgod drew nearer and nearer the birch tree. Finally it dawned on him quite clearly that he was on his way to see her, and his heart began to dance for joy. It had been a long time. The birch tree might well be missing him; in fact, the more he thought about it the surer he felt it was so. If it was really so, then he was very sorry for having neglected her. His heart danced as he strode on through the grass. But before long his stride faltered and he stopped dead; a great, blue wave of sadness had suddenly washed over him. The fox was there before him. It was quite dark by now, but he could hear the fox's voice coming through the mist, which was glowing in the vague light of the moon.

"Why, of course," he was saying, "Just because something agrees with the laws of symmetry is not to say that it is beautiful. That's nothing more than a dead beauty."

"How right you are!" came the birch tree's soft voice.

"True beauty is not something rigid and fossilized. People talk of observing the laws of symmetry, but it's enough if only the spirit of symmetry is present."

"Oh, yes, I'm sure it is," came the birch tree's gentle voice again.

This time the earthgod felt as though red flames were licking over his whole body. His breath came in short gasps, and he really thought he could bear it no longer. "What are you so miserable about?" he asked himself crossly. "What is it after all but a bit of talk between a birch tree and a fox in the open country? Do you call yourself a god, to let such things upset you?" But the fox was talking again, ". . . so all books on art touch on this aspect."

"Do you have many books on art, then?" asked the birch tree.

"Oh, not such an enormous number. I suppose I have most of them in English, German, and Japanese. There's a newer one in Italian, but it hasn't come yet."

"How *fine* your library must be!"

"No, no. Just a few scattered volumes, you know. And besides, I use it for my studies too, so it's really an awful mess, what with a microscope in one corner, and the London *Times* lying over there, and a marble bust of Caesar here . . ."

"Oh, but how splendid! Really *splendid*!"

There was a little sniff from the fox that might have been either modesty or pride, then everything was still for a while.

By now the earthgod was quite beside himself. From what the fox said, it seemed he was actually more distinguished than the earthgod himself. He could no longer console himself with the thought that he was a god if nothing else. It was frightful. He felt like rushing over and tearing the fox in two. He told himself that one should never even think such things. But then, what was he to do? Hadn't he let the fox get the better of him? He clutched at his breast in distress.

"Hasn't the telescope you once mentioned come yet?" started the birch tree again.

"The telescope I mentioned?—oh, no, it hasn't come yet. I keep expecting it, but the shipping routes are terribly busy. As soon as it comes, I'll bring it for you to see. I really must show you the rings round Venus, for one thing. They're so beautiful."

At this, the earthgod clapped his hands over his ears and rushed off to the north like an arrow from a bow. He had suddenly felt frightened at the thought of what he might do if he stayed silent there any longer.

He ran on and on in a straight line. When he finally collapsed out of breath he found himself at the foot of Mt. Mitsumori.

He rolled about in the grass, tearing at his hair. Then he began to cry in a loud voice. The sound rose up into the sky, where it echoed like thunder out of season and made itself heard all over the plain. He wept and wept until dawn, when, tired out, he finally wandered vacantly back to his shrine.

❧

Time passed, and autumn came at last. The birch tree was still green, but on the grass round about, the golden ears were already formed and glinting in the breeze, and here and there the berries of the lily of the valley showed ripe and red.

One transparent gold autumn day found the earthgod in the very best of tempers. All the unpleasant things he had been feeling since the summer seemed somehow to have dissolved into a kind of mist that hovered in only the vaguest of rings over his head. The odd, cross-grained streak in him had quite disappeared, too. He felt that if the birch tree wanted to talk to the fox—well, she could, and that if the two of them enjoyed talking together, it was a very good thing for them both. He would let the birch tree know how he felt today. With a light heart and his head full of such thoughts, the earthgod set off walking in the direction of the birch tree.

The birch tree saw him coming in the distance, and as ever trembled anxiously as she waited for him to arrive.

The earthgod came up and greeted her cheerfully.

"Good morning, Birch Tree. A lovely day we're having!"

"Good morning, Earthgod. Yes, it's a lovely day."

"What a blessing the sun is, to be sure! There he is up there, red in the spring, white in the summer, and golden in the autumn; and when he turns golden in the autumn, the grapes turn purple. Ah, a blessing indeed!"

"How true!"

"D'ye know—today I feel much better. I've had all sorts of trials since the summer, but this morning at last something suddenly lifted from my mind."

The birch tree wanted to reply, but for some reason a great weight seemed to be bearing down on her, and she remained silent.

"The way I feel now, I'd willingly die for anybody. I'd even take the place of a worm if it had to die and didn't want to." He gazed into the blue sky in the distance as he spoke, his eyes dark and splendid.

Again the birch tree wanted to reply, but again something heavy seemed to weigh her down, and she barely managed a sigh.

It was then that the fox appeared.

25

When the fox saw the earthgod there, he started and turned pale. But he could hardly go back, so he came out, trembling slightly, right up to where the birch tree stood.

"Good morning, Birch Tree," said the fox. "I believe that's the earthgod over there, no?" He was wearing his light brown leather shoes and a brown raincoat and was still in his summer hat.

"I'm the earthgod, lovely weather, isn't it?" The earthgod spoke, without a shadow on his mind.

"I must apologize for coming when you have a visitor," said the fox to the birch tree, his face pale with jealousy. "Here's the book I promised you the other day. Oh, and the telescope—I'll show you it one evening when the sky is clear. Goodbye."

"Oh, thank you..." began the birch tree, but the fox had already set off towards home without so much as a nod to the earthgod. The birch tree went suddenly pale and began to quiver again.

For a while, the earthgod gazed vacantly after the fox's retreating form. Then the sun suddenly glinted on the fox's brown leather shoes under the grass, and he came to himself with a start. The next moment something seemed to click in his brain. The fox was marching steadily into the distance, swaggering almost defiantly as he went. The earthgod began to seethe with rage. His face turned a dreadful black color. He'd show him what was what—that fox with his art books and his telescope!

He was up and after the fox in a flash. The birch tree's branches began to shake all at once in panic. Sensing something wrong, the fox himself glanced round equally, only to see the earthgod, black all over, rushing after him like a hurricane. Off went the fox like the wind, his face white and his mouth twisted with fear.

To the earthgod, the grass about him seemed to be flitting the white line. Even the shining blue sky had suddenly become a yawning black pit with crimson flame blazing and roaring in its depths.

They ran shouting and panting like two railway trains. The fox ran as in a dream, and all the while of his brain kept saying, "This is the end. This is the end. Telescope, Telescope, Telescope..."

A small hummock of bare earth lay ahead. The fox dashed round it so as to get to the round hole at its base. He ducked his head and was diving into the hole, his back legs flailing up as he went, when the earthgod finally pounced on him.

When the fox saw the earthgod there, he started and turned pale. But he could hardly go back, so he came on, trembling slightly, right up to where the birch tree stood.

"Good morning, Birch Tree," said the fox. "I believe that's the earthgod I see there, isn't it?" He was wearing his light brown leather shoes and a brown raincoat and was still in his summer hat.

"I'm the earthgod. Lovely weather, isn't it?" The earthgod spoke without a shadow on his mind.

"I must apologize for coming when you have a visitor," said the fox to the birch tree, his face pale with jealousy. "Here's the book I promised you the other day. Oh, and the telescope—I'll show you it one evening when the sky's clear. Goodbye."

"Oh, *thank* you . . ." began the birch tree, but the fox had already set off towards home without so much as a nod to the earthgod. The birch tree went suddenly pale and began to quiver again.

For a while, the earthgod gazed vacantly after the fox's retreating form. Then the sun suddenly glinted on the fox's brown leather shoes amidst the grass, and he came to himself with a start. The next moment, something seemed to click in his brain. The fox was marching steadily into the distance, swaggering almost defiantly as he went. The earthgod began to seethe with rage. His face turned a dreadful black color. He'd show him what was what—that fox with his art books and his telescopes!

He was up and after the fox in a flash. The birch tree's branches began to shake all at once in panic. Sensing something wrong, the fox himself glanced round casually, only to see the earthgod, black all over, rushing after him like a hurricane. Off went the fox like the wind, his face white and his mouth twisted with fear.

To the earthgod, the grass about him seemed to be burning like white fire. Even the shining blue sky had suddenly become a yawning black pit with crimson flames burning and roaring in its depths.

They ran snorting and panting like two railway trains. The fox ran as in a dream, and all the while part of his brain kept saying, "This is the end. This is the end. Telescope. Telescope. Telescope . . ."

A small hummock of bare earth lay ahead. The fox dashed round it so as to get to the round hole at its base. He ducked his head, and was diving into the hole, his back legs flicking up as he went, when the earthgod finally pounced on him from behind. The next moment he lay all twisted, with his head drooping life-lessly over the earthgod's hand and his lips puckered as though smiling slightly.

The earthgod flung the fox down on the ground and stamped on his soft, yielding body some four or five times. Then he plunged into the fox's hole. It was quite bare and dark, though the red clay of the floor had been trodden down hard and neat.

The earthgod went outside again, feeling rather strange, with his mouth all slack and twisted. Next, he tried putting a hand inside the pocket of the fox's raincoat as he lay there dead and limp. The pocket contained two brown burrs, of the kind foxes comb their fur with. From the earthgod's open mouth came the most extraordinary sound, and he burst into tears.

The tears fell like rain on the fox, and the fox lay there dead, with his head lolling limper and limper and the faintest of smiles on his face.

The Bears of Mt. Nametoko

The bears of Mt. Nametoko are worth hearing about. Mt. Nametoko is a large mountain, and the Fuchizawa River starts somewhere inside it. On most days of the year, Mt. Nametoko breathes in and breathes out cold mists and clouds. The mountains all about it, too, are like blackish green sea slugs or bald sea goblins. Halfway up the mountain there yawns a great cave, from which the river Fuchizawa falls suddenly some three hundred feet in a waterfall that goes thundering down through the thick-growing cypresses and maples.

Nowadays nobody walks along the old Nakayama Highway, so it is all grown over with butterbur and knotweed, and there are places where people have put up fences on the track to stop cattle from getting away and climbing up the mountains. But if you push your way for about six miles through the rustling undergrowth, you will hear in the distance a sound like the wind on a mountain-top. If you peer carefully in that direction, you might be puzzled by something long, white, and narrow that comes falling down the mountain in a flurry of mist. Those are the Ozora Falls of Mt. Nametoko. And in that area, they say, there used to be any number of bears. To tell the truth, I myself have never seen either Mt. Nametoko or the liver of a newly killed bear. This is all what I have heard from others, or worked out for myself. It may not be entirely true, but I, at least, believe it.

What is certain, at any rate, is that Mt. Nametoko is famous for its bear's liver. It is good for the stomach-ache and it helps wounds to heal. At the entrance to the Namari hot springs there is a sign that says Bear's Liver From Mt. Nametoko. So it is certain that there are bears on Mt. Nametoko. I can almost see them, going across the valleys with their pink tongues lolling out, and the bear cubs wrestling with each other till finally they lose their tempers and box each other's ears. It was those same bears that the celebrated bear hunter Kojuro Fuchizawa once killed so freely.

Kojuro Fuchizawa was a swarthy, well-knit, middle-aged man with a squint. His body was massive, like a small barrel, and his hands were as big and thick

as the handprint of the god Bishamon that they use to cure people's sicknesses at the Kitajima Shrine. In summer, he wore a cape made of bark to keep off the rain, with leggings, and he carried a woodsman's axe and a gun as big and heavy as an old-fashioned blunderbuss. With his great yellow hound, he would crisscross the mountains from Mt. Nametoko to Shidoke Valley, from Mistumata to Mt. Sakkai, from Mamiana Wood to Shira Valley.

When he went up the old, dried-up valleys, the trees grew so thickly that it was like going through a shadowy green tunnel, though sometimes it suddenly became bright with green and gold, and at other times sunlight fell all around as though the whole place had burst into bloom. Kojuro walked slowly and ponderously, as completely at home as though he were in his own living room. The hound ran on ahead, scampering along high banks or plunging into the water. He would swim for all he was worth across the sluggish, faintly menacing backwaters, then, when he finally reached the other side, would shake himself vigorously to get the water out of his coat and stand with nose wrinkled waiting for his master to catch up. Kojuro would come across with his mouth slightly twisted, moving his legs stiffly and cautiously like a pair of compasses, while the water splashed up above his knees in a white frieze. And I should also add that the bears in the area of Mt. Nametoko were fond of Kojuro.

One proof of this is that they would often look down in silence from some high place as Kojuro squelched his way up the valleys or went along the narrow ledges, all grown over with thistles, that bordered the valley. Clinging to a branch at the top of a tree or sitting on the top of a bank with their paws round their knees, they would watch with interest as he went by.

The bears even seemed to like Kojuro's hound.

Yet for all that, they did not like it much when they really came up against Kojuro, and the dog flew at them like a ball of fire, or when Kojuro with a strange glint in his eyes leveled his gun at them. At such times, most bears would wave their paws as though in distress, telling him that they did not want to be treated in that way.

But there are all kinds of bears, just as there are all kinds of people, and the fiercer of them would rear up on their hind legs with a great roar and advance on Kojuro with both paws stretched out, ignoring the dog as though they could crush it underfoot as easily as that. Kojuro would remain perfectly calm and, taking aim at the center of the bear's forehead from behind a tree, would let fly with his gun.

30

The whole forest would seem to cry out loud, and the bear would slump to the ground. The dark red blood would gush from its mouth, it would snuffle rapidly, and it would die.

Then Kojuro would stand his gun against a tree, cautiously go up to the bear, and say something like this:

"Don't think I killed you out of hatred, Bear. I have to make a living, just as you have to be shot. I'd like to do different work, work with no sin attached, but I've no fields, and they say my trees belong to the authorities, and when I go into the village nobody will have anything to do with me. I'm a hunter because I can't help it. It's fate that made you a bear, and it's fate that makes me do this work. Make sure you're not reborn as a bear next time!"

At such times the dog, too, would sit by him with narrowed eyes and a dejected air.

The dog, you see, was Kojuro's sole companion. In the summer of his fortieth year, his whole family had fallen sick with dysentery, and his son and his son's wife had died. The dog, however, had remained healthy and vigorous.

Next, Kojuro would take out of his pocket a short, razor-sharp knife and in one long stroke slit the bear's skin open from under its chin down to its chest and on to its belly. The scene that followed I don't care to think about. Either way, in the end Kojuro would put the bright red bear's liver in the wooden chest on his back, wash the fur that was all in dripping, bloody tassels in the river, roll it up, put it on his back, and set off down the valley with a heavy heart.

It even seemed to Kojuro that he could understand what the bears were saying to each other. Early one spring, before any of the trees had turned green, Kojuro took the dog with him and went far up the marshy bed of the Shira Valley. As dusk drew near, he started to climb up to the pass leading over to Bakkai Valley, where he had built a small hut of bamboo grass to shelter in. But for some unexplained reason Kojuro, unlike his accustomed self, took the wrong trail. Any number of times he started up, then came down and started up again; even the dog was quite exhausted, and Kojuro himself was breathing heavily out of one side of his mouth before they finally found the previous year's hut, which was half tumbled down.

Remembering that there had been a spring just below the hut, Kojuro started

off down the mountain, but had only gone a little way when to his surprise he came across two bears, a mother and a cub barely a year old, standing in the faint light of the still new moon, staring intently at the other side of the valley with their paws up to their foreheads, just as a human being does when he is looking into the distance. To Kojuro it seemed almost that the two bears were surrounded by a kind of halo, and he stopped and stared at them transfixed.

Then the small bear said in a wheedling voice, "I'm sure it's snow, Mother. Only the near side of the valley is white, isn't it? Yes, I'm sure it's snow, Mother!"

The mother bear went on staring intently for a while, then said finally, "It's not snow. It wouldn't fall just in that one place."

"Then it must have been left there after the rest melted," said the cub.

"No, I went past there only yesterday on my way to look at the thistle buds."

Kojuro stared hard in the same direction. The moonlight was gliding bluish white down the mountainside, which was shining like a silver helmet. After a while the cub spoke again.

"If it's not snow then it must be frost. I'm sure it is."

There really will be a frost tonight, thought Kojuro to himself. A star was shimmering blue close to the moon; even the color of the moon itself was just like ice.

"I know what it is," said the mother bear. "It's cherry blossoms."

"Is that all? I know all about that."

"No, you've never seen it."

"But I *do* know it. I went and brought some home myself the other day."

"No—that wasn't cherry. It was Indian beech you brought home, I think."

"Really?" the cub said innocently.

For some reason, Kojuro's heart felt full. He gave a last glance at the flowers like snow on the far side of the valley, and at the mother bear and her cub standing bathed in the moonlight, then stealthily, taking care to make no sound, set off back. As he slowly withdrew, praying all the while that the wind would not blow his scent in their direction, the fragrance of spicebush came sharply to him on the moonlight.

Yet how pitifully humbled was that same brave Kojuro when he went to town to sell the bear skins and the bear liver.

Somewhere near the center of the town there was a large hardware store where winnowing baskets and sugar, whetstones and cheap cigarettes and even glass fly traps were set out for sale.

Kojuro had only to step over the threshold of the shop with the great bundle of bearskins on his back for the people there to start smiling as though to say, "Here he is again." The master of the shop would be seated massively beside a large brazier in a room leading off the shop.

"Thank you for your kindness last time, sir." And the same Kojuro who back in the hills was so completely his own master would set down his bundle of skins and, kneeling on the boards, bow deferentially.

"Well, well . . . And what can I do for you today?"

"I've brought along a few bearskins again."

"Bearskins? The last ones are still lying around somewhere in the store. We don't need any today."

"Don't be so difficult. Please buy some. I'll let you have them cheap."

"However cheap they are, I don't want them," the master of the shop would say with perfect composure, tapping out the small bowl of his pipe against the palm of his hand.

Whenever he heard this, Kojuro, brave lord of the hills, would feel his face twist with anxiety.

At Kojuro's home they could find chestnuts in the hills, and millet would grow in the apology for a field that lay at the back of the house; but no rice would grow, nor was there any soybean paste for making soup. So he must have some rice, however little, to take back for the family of seven—his old mother and his grandchildren.

If he had lived down in the village, he would have grown hemp for weaving cloth, but at Kojuro's place nothing grew but a few wisteria vines, which were woven into baskets and the like.

After a while, Kojuro would say in a voice hoarse with distress, "Please—please buy some, whatever the price." And Kojuro would actually bow to him again.

The shopkeeper would puff smoke for a while without saying anything, then concealing a slight grin of satisfaction would say, "Right. Leave them here. Heisuke, give Kojuro two yen, will you?"

Heisuke, who worked in the shop, would seat himself in front of Kojuro and hand him four large silver coins. Kojuro would accept with a grin and raise

them respectfully to his forehead. Then the master of the shop would gradually unbend.

"Here—give Kojuro some saké."

By now Kojuro would be glowing with delight. The shopkeeper would talk to him at leisure of this and that. Very deferentially, Kojuro would tell him of things back in the hills. Soon, word would come from the kitchen that the saké was ready. Kojuro would half make to go, but in the end would be dragged off to the kitchen, where he would go through his polite greetings again.

Almost immediately, they would bring a small black lacquered table bearing slices of salted salmon with chopped cuttlefish and a china bottle of warm saké.

Kojuro would seat himself very correctly and formally before the table. Then he would start to eat, balancing the pieces of cuttlefish on the back of his hand before gulping them down and reverently pouring the yellowish saké into the tiny cup.

However low prices might be, anyone would have agreed that two yen was too little for a pair of bear furs.

It was really too little, and Kojuro knew it. Why, then, did Kojuro not sell his furs to someone other than that hardware dealer? To most people, it would be a mystery. But in those days there was an order of things—it was laid down that Kojuro should get the better of the bears, that the shopkeeper should get the better of Kojuro, and that the bears—but since the shopkeeper lived in the town, the bears did not get the better of him, for the moment at least.

Such being the state of affairs, Kojuro killed the bears without any feeling of hatred for them. One year, though, a strange thing happened.

Kojuro was squelching his way up a valley and had climbed onto a rock to look about him when he saw a large bear, its back hunched, clambering like a cat up a tree directly in front of him. Immediately, Kojuro leveled his gun. The dog, delighted, was already at the foot of the tree, rushing round and round it madly.

But the bear, who for a while seemed to be debating whether he should come down and set on Kojuro or let himself be shot where he was, suddenly let go with his paws and came crashing down to the ground. Immediately on his guard, Kojuro put his gun to his shoulder and went closer as though to shoot. But at this

34

point the bear put up its paws and shouted, "What are you after? Why do you have to shoot me?"

"For nothing but your fur and your liver," said Kojuro. "Not that I shall get any great sum for them when I take them to town. I'm very sorry for you, but it just can't be helped. But when I hear you say that kind of thing, I almost feel I'd rather live on chestnuts and ferns and the like, even if it killed me."

"Won't you wait two more years? For myself, I don't care whether I die or not, but there are still things I must do, so wait just two years. When two years are up, you'll find me dead in front of your house without fail. You can have my fur, and my insides too."

Filled with an odd emotion, Kojuro stood quite still, thinking.

The bear got its four paws firmly on the ground and began, ever so slowly, to walk. But still Kojuro went on standing there, staring vacantly in front of him.

Slowly, slowly, the bear walked away without looking back, as though it knew very well that Kojuro would never let fly suddenly from behind. For a moment, its broad, brownish black back shone bright in the sunlight falling through the branches of the trees, and at that same moment Kojuro gave a painful groan and, crossing the valley, made for home.

It was just two years later. One morning, the wind blew so fiercely that Kojuro, sure that it was blowing down trees and hedge and all, went outside to see. The cypress hedge was standing untouched, but at its foot there lay something brownish black that he had seen before. His heart gave a turn, for it was just two years, and he had been feeling worried in case the bear should come along. He went up to it, and found the bear he had met that day, lying there as it had promised, dead, in a great pool of blood that had gushed from its mouth. Almost unconsciously, Kojuro pressed his hands together in prayer.

It was one day in January. As Kojuro was leaving home that morning, he said something he had never said before.

"Mother, I must be getting old. This morning, for the first time in my life, I don't feel I want to wade through the streams."

Kojuro's mother of ninety-one, who sat spinning on the veranda in the sun, raised her rheumy eyes and glanced at Kojuro with an expression that might have been either tearful or smiling.

Kojuro tied on his straw sandals, heaved himself to his feet, and set off. One after the other the children poked their faces out of the barn and said smiling, "Come home soon, Grandpa."

Kojuro looked up at the smooth, bright blue sky, then turned to his grandchildren and said, "I'll be back later."

He climbed up through the pure white, close-packed snow in the direction of Shira Valley. The dog was already panting heavily, its pink tongue lolling out as it ran ahead and stopped, ran ahead and stopped again. Very soon Kojuro's figure sank out of sight beyond a low hill, and the children returned to their games.

Kojuro followed the bank of the river up the Shira Valley. Here the water lay in deep blue pools, there it was frozen into sheets of glass, here the icicles hung in countless numbers like bead curtains, and from both banks the berries of the spindletree peered out like red and yellow flowers. As he climbed upstream, Kojuro saw his own glittering shadow and the dog's, deep indigo and sharply etched on the snow, mingling as they moved with the shadows of the birch trunks.

On the other side of the summit from Shira Valley there lived, as he had confirmed during the summer, a large bear.

On he went upstream, fording five small tributaries that came flowing into the valley, crossing the water again and again from right to left and from left to right. He came to a small waterfall, from the foot of which he began to climb up towards the ridge. The snow was so dazzling it seemed to be on fire, and as he toiled upward, Kojuro felt as if he had purple glasses before his eyes.

The dog was climbing as though determined that the steepness of the slope would not beat him, clinging grimly to the snow, though he nearly slipped many times. When they finally reached the top they found themselves on a plateau that sloped gently away, where the snow sparkled like white marble and snow-covered peaks thrust up into the sky all about them.

It happened as Kojuro was taking a rest there at the summit. Suddenly, the dog began to bark frantically. Startled, Kojuro looked behind him and saw the same great bear that he had glimpsed that summer rearing up on its hind legs and bearing down on him. Without panic, Kojuro planted his feet firmly in the snow and took aim.

Raising its two massive front paws, the bear came rushing straight at him. Even Kojuro turned rather pale at the sight.

36

Kojuro heard the crack of the gun. Yet the bear showed no sign of falling, but seemed to come swaying on towards him, black and raging like a storm. The dog sank his teeth into its leg. The next moment, a great noise filled Kojuro's head and everything about him went white. Then, far off in the distance, he heard a voice saying, "Ah, Kojuro, I didn't mean to kill you."

"This is death," thought Kojuro. All about him he could see light twinkling incessantly like blue stars. "Those are the signs that I'm dead," he thought, "the fires you see when you die. Forgive me, bears." As for what he felt from then on, I have no idea.

It was the evening of the third day following. A moon hung in the sky like a great ball of ice. The snow was a bright bluish white, and the water gave off a phosphorescent glow. The Pleiades and Orion's belt twinkled now green, now orange, as though they were breathing.

On the plateau on top of the mountain, surrounded by chestnut trees and snowy peaks, many great black shapes were gathered in a ring, each casting its own black shadow, each prostrate in the snow like a Muslim at prayer, never moving. And there at the highest point one might have seen, by the light of the snow and the moon, Kojuro's corpse set in a kneeling position. One might even have imagined that on Kojuro's dead, frozen face one could see a chill smile as though he were still alive. And Orion's belt moved to the center of the heavens, it tilted still further to the west, yet the great black shapes stayed quite still, as though they had turned to stone.

Brush drawing, *Snow and Pines*

The Spider, the Slug, and the Raccoon

A red spider with long arms and a silver-colored slug and a raccoon who had never washed his face all started at the Badger School together. There were three things that Mr. Badger taught.

First, he taught about the race between the tortoise and the hare. Next, he taught that, as this showed, it was up to everyone to overtake his fellows and become bigger and more important than they. The third thing was that the biggest person was the most worthy of all.

From then on the three of them worked with all their might, vying with each other to be top of the class.

In the first grade, the slug and the raccoon were punished for always being late, so the spider came out on top. The slug and the raccoon shed tears of mortification.

In the second grade, Mr. Badgar made a mistake in calculating his marks, so the slug came first. The spider and the raccoon ground their teeth in mortification.

In the third grade examination, the light was so bright that it made Mr. Badger's eyes water and he kept shutting them. So the raccoon looked into the textbook as he wrote the answers and came first.

Thus the red spider with long arms and the silver slug and the raccoon who had never washed his face all graduated from Mr. Badger's school at the same time.

The three of them, who were very good friends on the surface, did all kinds of things to mark the occasion. They held a party for Mr. Badger to thank him for his kindness, followed by a special farewell party for themselves, but deep in their hearts they were all busy thinking about each other and saying to themselves, "Pooh! And what good do they think *they* are? Just wait and see who becomes the biggest and most important!"

Once the meetings were over, they all went back to their own homes to put the things they had learned into practice. Mr. Badger was already busy again, chasing a sewer rat every day in order to enroll him in school.

Just about this time the dogtooth violets were in bloom, and innumerable blue-eyed bees were flying about cheerfully, buzzing in the sunlight, giving greetings to each small flower in turn before they took its honey and scent, or carrying the golden balls of pollen to other flowers for them in return, or collecting the wax that the new buds on the trees had no more need of, so as to build their six-sided homes. It was a busy, cheerful day at the beginning of spring.

What Befell the Spider

The evening after the parties were over the spider came back to the oak tree where he lived at the entrance to the wood.

Unfortunately, he had used up all his money at the Badger School, and he had not a single thing of his own. So he put up with his hunger and began to spin a web beneath the dim light of the moon.

He was so hungry that he had hardly any web left in his body. But he muttered to himself "They'll see! They'll see!" and spun out the thread for all he was worth, till at last he had spun a web about as big as a small copper coin. Then he hid himself behind a branch and all night long peered out at the web with gleaming eyes.

Around dawn, a baby horsefly came flying along humming to himself and ran into the web. But the spider had been so hungry when he spun the web that the thread was not a bit sticky, and the baby horsefly had soon broken it and was making to fly away.

Quite beside himself, the spider rushed out from behind the branch and sank his teeth into the horsefly.

"Mercy! Mercy!" wept the little horsefly piteously, but without saying anything the spider ate him up, head, wings, feet and all. He heaved a satisfied sigh and for a while lay looking up at the sky and rubbing his belly, then he produced a little more thread. So the web grew one size bigger.

The spider went back behind the branch, and his six eyes gleamed bright as he sat motionless, watching the web.

"Where would this be, now?" inquired a blind mayfly who came along, walking with the aid of a stick.

"This is an inn, sir," said the spider, blinking all his six eyes separately.

The mayfly seated himself in the web with an air of weariness. The spider ran out.

"Here's some tea for you," he said, and without warning sank his teeth into the mayfly's body.

The mayfly raised the hand with which he had been going to take the tea and threshed about helplessly, at the same time beginning to recite in a piteous voice:

> Ah, pity on my daughter when
> The dreadful tidings drear . . .

"Here, that's enough of that row! Stop your struggling!" said the spider, whereupon the mayfly pressed his palms together and entreated him, "Have pity, kind sir. Pray wait a while, that I may recite my last poem."

"All right, but be quick!" said the spider, feeling a little sorry for him. And he waited, keeping a firm grip on the mayfly's legs.

The mayfly began to recite in a truly pitiful, tiny voice, going back to the beginning of the poem and starting all over again:

> Ah, pity on my daughter when
> The dreadful tidings drear
> Of parent's doom so far from home
> Shall reach her sorrowing ear!
> Most pitiful a pilgrim's staff
> She'll take in her small hand,
> And on a weary pilgrimage
> She'll set off through the land.
> A-wandering from door to door
> Through wind and rain she goes.
> "Oh, give me alms," she begs, "that I
> May pray his soul's repose."
> Dear Daughter, be forewarned and shun
> The cruel spider's lair.
> Of this my last advice take heed—
> Of webby inns beware!

"Enough of your impudence!" exclaimed the spider, and swallowed the mayfly in one gulp. For a while he lay looking up at the sky and rubbing his belly, then he gave a wink, sang playfully to himself, "Now your days of impudence are over," and started spinning thread again.

The web grew three sizes larger, so that it was like a splendid, large umbrella. Quite easy in his mind by now, the spider hid himself again in the leaves. Just then, he heard someone singing in a pleasant voice down below:

> O, the red long-legged spider
> Crawls about up in the sky
> As he lets out, soft and bright,
> His silver thread of light
> In a shining web spun high.

He looked and saw it was a pretty female spider.

"Come up here," said the long-armed spider, letting a long, long thread of web down for her.

The female spider got hold of it at once and came climbing up. So the two of them became man and wife. There were all kinds of things to eat in the web every day, and the wife spider ate a great deal and turned it all into babies. So lots of baby spiders were born. But they were all so small you could hardly see them.

It was terribly lively, with the children sliding on the web, and wrestling, and swinging. And best of all, the dragonfly came one day and informed them that the insects had passed a resolution making the spider vice-president of the Society of Insects and Worms.

One day, the spider and his wife were hidden in the leaves drinking tea when they heard someone singing down below in a conceited voice:

> O, the red long-legged spider,
> Of sons he had ten score,
> But the biggest of them all
> Was incredibly small—
> Like a grain of sand, no more.

They looked and found it was the silver slug, who had grown tremendously big since they last saw him.

The spider's good lady was so put out that she cried and cried and would not be consoled.

But the long-armed spider sniffed and said, "He's jealous of me these days, that's what. Ho! Slug—I'm being made vice-president of the Society of Insects and Worms! How d'you like that, eh? I can't see the likes of you doing that, however fat you may get. Ha, ha, ha, ha! . . ."

The slug was so furious that he came down with a fever for several days and could say nothing but, "Ah, that cursed spider! Such an insult! That cursed spider!"

From time to time the web would break in the wind or would be damaged by some lout of a stag beetle, but the spider soon spun out a smooth length of thread and mended it again.

Of their two hundred children, a full one hundred and ninety-eight were carried off by ants, or disappeared without trace, or died of dysentery. But the children were all so much alike that their parents soon forgot all about them.

And the web by now was a magnificent affair. A steady stream of insects got caught in it.

One day, the spider and his wife were again hidden in the leaves drinking tea when a traveling mosquito came flying along, took one look at the web, and flew away again in alarm. The spider put three of its legs out into the net and watched in disgust as it went.

Just then, a great peal of laughter came from down below, and a rich voice began to sing:

> O, red long-legged spider,
> Long-legged spider red—
> Your web is such a poor affair
> The traveling mosquito there
> Just hummed and turned his head.

It was the raccoon who had never washed his face.

"You wait, fool Raccoon!" said the spider, gnashing his teeth in rage. "Before long I'll be president of the Society of Insects and Worms and then I'll have you bowing to me—you wait and see!"

From then on, the spider set to work furiously. He spun a full ten webs in different places and kept watch over them even at night.

But sad to tell, the rot set in. So much food piled up that in time things began to go bad. And the rot spread to the spider and his wife and their children. All four of them began to rot and turn soggy, beginning at the ends of their legs, till one day they were finally washed away by the rain.

This was around the time when the pearlwort was in bloom, and the many blue-eyed bees had scattered over the countryside, where they gathered the honey from each small flower as though taking fire from small handlamps.

What Befell the Silver Slug

Around the time when the spider spun his copper-coin web on the oak tree at the entrance to the wood, a stag beetle turned up at the silver slug's fine residence.

By then, the slug had quite a reputation in the wood. He was educated, everyone said, and he was good-natured and considerate to others.

"Slug," said the stag beetle, "I'm going through hard times now. There's nothing for me to eat, and no water, so I wonder if you'd let me have just a little of the butterbur juice you've got stored?"

"Why, of course I will," said the slug. "Come inside, won't you?"

"That's very kind of you. You're a friend in need," said the stag beetle as he gulped down the butterbur juice.

"Have some more," said the slug. "Why, in a way we're brothers. Ho, ho, ho! Come on, now, just a little more."

"Well, then, perhaps just a little. Thank you, thank you." And the stag beetle drank a little more.

"Beetle," said the slug. "When you feel better, shall we have a little wrestle? We haven't wrestled for ages. Ho, ho, ho! Not for ages."

"I'm too starved to have the strength," said the stag beetle.

"Then I'll give you something to eat. Here, help yourself," said the slug, getting out some thistle buds and the like.

"Most kind. Since you insist then . . ." And the beetle ate them.

"Now let's wrestle. Ho, ho, ho," said the slug, getting up as he spoke.

"I'm afraid I'm rather weak," said the stag beetle, getting up reluctantly, "so please don't throw me too heavily."

"Heave-ho! There!" The beetle hit the ground with a crash. "Once more, eh? Ho, ho, ho!"

"No, I'm tired now."

"Oh, come on! Heave-ho! There! Ho, ho, ho!" Again the beetle crashed to the floor.

"Once more. Ho, ho, ho!"

"No, I've had enough."

"Come on, now, just once. Heave-*ho*! Oh, ho, ho, ho . . ." Crash went the beetle again.

"Once more. Ho, ho, ho!"

"No, I'm . . ."

"Oh, come on! Heave-ho! Ho, ho, ho, ho!" Crash went the beetle.

"Once more."

"I'm dying. Goodbye."

"Come on, now. Just once. Ho, ho, ho. . . . Come now, on your feet! Here, let me help you up. Heave-ho! There! Ho, ho, ho, ho . . ."

And the beetle died. So the silver slug munched him down, the hard outside parts and all.

About a month after that, a lizard came limping along to the slug's splendid residence.

"Slug," he said, "I wonder if I could have a little medicine today?"

"What's wrong?" asked the slug with a smile.

"I've been bitten by a snake," said the lizard.

"Oh, that's easy," said the slug, smiling. "I'll just give it a little lick for you. If I lick it the snake poison will soon disappear. It ought to, seeing that I can dissolve the snake itself. Ho, ho, ho!"

"I'd be most grateful, then," said the lizard, putting out his leg.

"Why, of course, of course. We're brothers in a way, aren't we? And so are you and the snake, eh? Ho, ho, ho!" And the slug put his mouth to the lizard's wound.

"Thank you, Slug," said the lizard after a while.

"I must lick it some more yet, or you'll suffer later. I won't make it better if you come here asking again. Ho, ho, ho!" mumbled the slug indistinctly as he went on licking the lizard.

"Slug," said the lizard in alarm, "I do believe my leg's starting to dissolve!"

"Ho, ho, ho! Why, it's nothing much," replied the slug indistinctly as before. "Ho, ho, ho!"

"Slug—" said the lizard anxiously. "I'm feeling kind of hot around the middle."

"Ho, ho, ho," mumbled the slug. "Why, it's nothing to fuss about."

"Slug," cried the lizard tearfully, "I do believe my body's half melted away. Stop now, please!"

"Ho, ho, ho! Why, it's nothing much at all," said the slug. "Just a very little. Ho, ho, ho!"

As he heard this, the lizard stopped worrying at last. He stopped worrying because it was just at that moment that his heart melted.

So the slug slupped up the lizard completely. And he became quite ridicu-

lously big. He had felt so pleased with himself that he hadn't been able to resist teasing the spider.

But the spider had taunted him in return, so that he had taken to his bed with a fever, and day after day he would say, "You just see. I'll get as big as I can, then I'll almost certainly be made an honorary member of the Society of Insects and Worms. And if the spider says anything, I won't answer but just give him a contemptuous sniff."

In fact, though, the slug's reputation, for some reason or other, began to decline just around then.

The raccoon in particular would always pooh-pooh any mention of the slug, saying with a smile, "I can't say I think much of the slug's way of doing things. Why, anybody could get big the way he does it!"

When the slug heard this he got still more angry and tried frantically to find ways of becoming an honorary society member as soon as possible.

Before long the spider rotted and dissolved and was washed away in the rain, so the slug felt a bit easier, though he was still waiting eagerly for someone to turn up.

Then one day a frog came along.

"Good day, Slug," he said. "Could you let me have a little water?"

"Nice to see you, Frog," said the slug in a determinedly pleasant voice, since he was longing to slup up the frog. "Water? As much as you like. There's been quite a drought lately, but you and I are brothers in a way, aren't we? Ho, ho, ho!" He took the frog to the water jar.

The frog drank his fill, then he looked at the slug for a while with an innocent expression and said, "Slug, shall we have a wrestle?"

The slug was delighted. The frog had made the very suggestion that he had been about to make himself. A feeble creature like the frog would probably be ready for slupping up after five throws or so.

"Let's," he said. "Heave-ho! There! Ho, ho, ho!" The frog was dashed to the ground.

"Let's try again. Heave-ho! There! Ho, ho, ho!" Again the frog was thrown.

At this point the frog hastily got a bag of salt out of his pocket.

"Sumo wrestlers always purify the ring with salt," he said. "There!" And the ground all about was scattered with white salt.

"Frog," said the slug, "I'm sure you'll beat me next time. You're so strong. Heave-ho! There! Ho, ho, ho!" The frog was dashed to the ground.

48

He lay there spread-eagled, with his green belly turned up to the sky as though he were dead. The silver slug made to go to slup him up, but for some reason he couldn't move his legs. He looked, and found they were half dissolved.

"Heavens! The salt!" cried the slug.

At this the frog leaped up and, seating himself cross-legged on the ground, opened wide his great holdall of a mouth and laughed.

"Goodbye, Slug," he said with a bow. "This is most distressing for you."

The slug was nearly in tears.

"Frog," he said. "Goo . . ." But just then his tongue dissolved.

The frog laughed and laughed.

"I expect you were going to say goodbye," he said. "Well, goodbye to you then. When I get home, I'll have a good cry for you." And off he sped without looking back once.

The white flowers of the buckwheat sown in autumn were just beginning to bloom, and the countless blue-eyed bees were moving about among the pinkish stalks that filled the square field, swaying on the tiny branches that bore the flowers, busily gathering the last honey of the year.

What Befell the Raccoon

The raccoon did not wash his face on purpose.

By the time the spider had spun his first web the size of a copper coin on the oak at the entrance to the wood, the raccoon was back at the temple where he lived in the country. But he, too, was quite starved, and was leaning against a pine tree with his eyes closed when a rabbit came along.

"Raccoon," the rabbit said, "it's dreadful to be hungry like this. One might as well die and have done with it."

"Yes indeed," said the raccoon. "It's all up with us. But it is the will of Wildcat, the Blessed Feline. Ah, Ave Feles, Ave Feles!"

The rabbit joined him in reciting the Ave Feles.

"Ave Feles, Ave Feles, Ave Feles!" The raccoon took the rabbit's paw and drew him a little closer.

"Ave Feles, Ave Feles," murmured the raccoon. "Everything is the will of the Blessed Feline. Ave Feles, Ave Feles . . ." And he took a bite of the rabbit's ear.

"Ouch!" cried the rabbit in alarm. "Raccoon, what are you doing?"

"Ave Feles, Ave Feles," mumbled the raccoon, his mouth full of the rabbit's ear. "Everything on earth is ordained by the will of Wildcat. Ah, the ineffable wisdom that decrees that I should chew your ears down to a reasonable size! Ave Feles! . . ." And he finished by eating up both the rabbit's ears.

As he listened, the rabbit was gradually filled with joy and began to shed great tears.

"Ave Feles, Ave Feles! Ah, blessed be Wildcat! Ah, how great a love that troubles itself even with the ears of such wretches as I! What are two ears, or more, if only one be saved? Ave Feles!"

The raccoon, too, shed great false tears.

"Ave Feles, Ave Feles! Thou sayest to chew the rabbit's legs this time? That would be because he jumps too much, perhaps. Yes, yes—I chew, I chew! Ave Feles, Ave Feles! Thy will be done!" And he took a good mouthful of the rabbit's back legs.

"Ah, praise be!" cried the rabbit ever more joyfully. "Thanks to you, Wildcat, my back legs are gone and I need walk no more! Ah, praise be! Ave Feles. Ave Feles!"

The raccoon was pretending to cry as though his whole body would soon be soaked in tears.

"Ave Feles, Ave Feles! Everything is according to thy will. So thou sayest that a humble creature such as I must live on to carry out thy will? Very well, very well, if such be thy will. . . . Ave Feles, Ave Feles, Ave Feles! Thy will be done. Mumble, munch . . ."

The rabbit disappeared completely.

"You cheated me!" he called from the raccoon's stomach. "Your stomach is pitch dark! Ah, what a fool I was!"

"Stop that row!" said the raccoon angrily. "Hurry up and get digested!"

"Listen everybody!" the rabbit called again. "Don't be tricked by the raccoon!"

Peering anxiously around, the raccoon shut his mouth and kept it like that for a while, covering his nose with his paw at the same time so that the sound could not get out.

Just two months after this, the raccoon was performing the devotions as usual at his house when a wolf came carrying half a bushel of unhulled rice and begged him for a sermon.

"The lives that you have taken," began the raccoon, "will not be easily atoned

for. What living creature is there that dies willingly? But you ate them, did you not? Make haste to repent, else dire torment awaits you! Ah, how fearful! Ave Feles, Ave Feles!"

Terrified out of his wits, the wolf stared anxiously about him. "Then what do you think I should do?" he said.

"I am the representative of the Blessed Feline," said the raccoon. "So you must do as I say. Ave Feles, Ave Feles!"

"What must I do?" asked the wolf in alarm.

"Well, now," said the raccoon. "Just stay still, and I'll take your fangs out. Ah, how many innocent lives have these fangs taken! A fearful thing. Now I'll gouge out your eyes. How many creatures have these eyes stared into death! A dreadful thought. And now (Ave Feles, Ave Feles, Ave Feles!) I'll just chew your ears a little. This is by way of punishment. Ave Feles! Ave Feles! Bear up, now. Now I'll chew your head. Mumble, mumble. Ave Feles! The important thing in this world is endurance. Ave . . . mumble, munch . . . Now I'll eat your legs. Very tasty. Ave Feles, munch, mumble. Now your back . . . mm, this is good too. Mumble, mumble, munch, munch . . . "

In the end, the wolf was eaten up entirely. And he called out from inside the raccoon's stomach, "It's pitch dark in here. But here are some rabbit's bones. Who could have killed him? Whoever you are, I expect you'll be chewed up while listening to a sermon by the raccoon."

"You make too much noise," said the raccoon. "I must put a lid on you." And he swallowed whole the bundle containing half a bushel of rice that the wolf had brought with him.

The next day, though, the raccoon just didn't feel at all well. For some reason, his stomach hurt dreadfully, and he had a pricking feeling in his throat.

At first he eased the pain by drinking water, but it grew worse each successive day, till in the end he was beside himself with pain.

Finally, on the twenty-fifth day after he had eaten the wolf, the raccoon, whose body was swollen up like a rubber balloon by now, burst open with a great boom.

When all the animals in the wood gathered in alarm, they found that the raccoon's body was stuffed with rice plants. The rice that the raccoon had swallowed had sprouted and grown.

Mr. Badger came too, a little late. He took a look and said with a great yawn, "Dear me, what a great pity. All three of them were such clever children."

It was early winter by now, and each of the blue-eyed bees in the swarm was in the hexagonal home that he had made of wax, sleeping peacefully, dreaming of the spring to come.

A Stem of Lilies

"At seven tomorrow morning, they say, Shohenchi will cross the Himukya River and enter the town." So came the word on the clear breeze, spreading to all the houses in the walled town of Hamukya.

They were as happy as children; for who can say how earnestly and for how many years the people of the town had been longing for Shohenchi to come? Besides, many people from their town had gone to join Shohenchi and become his disciples.

"At seven tomorrow morning, they say, Shohenchi will cross the Himukya River and enter the town."

What kind of countenance would Shohenchi have, they wondered, and what color were his eyes? Would he have dark blue eyes like lotus petals, as it was rumored? Would the nails on his fingers truly gleam like copper? What would they have to say, the men who had gone to join him from the town, and how would they be dressed? . . . As gaily as children, the people set their houses in order, and when that was done they went out and thoroughly cleaned the streets. Here, there and, everywhere, they were to be seen outside their homes, sweeping the roadway. The surfaces were sprinkled with water, and the cow dung and stones all carefully removed, then the roads were strewn with white quartz sand.

"At seven tomorrow morning, they say, Shohenchi will cross the Himukya River and enter the town."

The news, of course, reached the royal palace in no time.

"Your Majesty, at seven tomorrow morning, they say, Shohenchi will cross the Himukya River and arrive here."

"Indeed! Are you certain?" demanded the king, forgetting himself so far as to rise from his throne inlaid with agate.

"It seems it is indeed so, sire. Two merchants of Hamura claim to have paid homage to him this very morning on the far bank of the Himukya."

"Indeed? Then it must be so. Ah, how long we have awaited him! Give the command at once that the town be cleaned."

53

"Sire, the town has already been thoroughly cleaned. So delighted were the people that they cleaned the streets thoroughly without awaiting your bidding."

The king grunted. "Go, even so, and make sure there have been no oversights. Then give word that food be prepared for a thousand persons."

"Very well, Your Majesty. The Master of the Royal Kitchens has been wandering up and down the kitchens for some time, impatiently awaiting Your Majesty's command."

"I see . . ." The king thought for a while. "Then the next thing is the holy lodgings. Go, now, and tell the carpenters to construct a lodging place for one thousand persons in the oak grove outside the walls."

"Very well, Your Majesty. Your Majesty is most thoughtful. Indeed, the carpenters have already set about surveying the forest, foreseeing just such a royal command."

"Indeed!" murmured the king in surprise. "The virtues of Shohenchi impart themselves to others as swiftly as the wind. Tomorrow morning, I will go in person to the bank of the Himukya River to greet him. Let the news be spread abroad. You are to come at five, at the break of day."

"Very well, Your Majesty." The white-bearded minister left the royal presence joyfully, his cheeks rosy like a child's with joy.

Dawn broke the next day.

Behind his curtains the king heard the soft footfall as his prime minister entered, and was up in a flash.

"Your Majesty—it is just five o'clock."

The king grunted. "I did not sleep all night," he said, "yet my whole being this morning is as fresh as crystal. What of the weather?" The king came out of his curtains and stretched himself up straight.

"Fine weather indeed, Your Majesty. The lapis lazuli on the south side of Mt. Sumeru can be seen as though through crystal. How handsome the Buddha Shohenchi will surely seem on such a day as this!"

"It is well. Is the town as spotless as it was yesterday?"

"Your Majesty, it is as the shore of Lake Anobudabu."

"Are the provisions ready?"

"All preparations are complete."

"And the construction work in the oak grove?"

"It will be ready without fail before the morning is over. It only remains to set in the windows and sweep it out."

The king set out for the banks of the Himukya River, taking the others with him.

The wind rustled, and the leaves glittered on the trees.

"By this wind one may tell that it is September," said the king.

"Indeed, Your Majesty. This is the transparent dust of autumn. It is like innumerable particles of glass."

"Are the lilies in bloom yet?"

"The buds have all formed. The sharp grains of the autumn wind are wearing away the gold fastenings at their tips. It seems likely that the flowers will all open together this morning."

"No doubt. I have a mind to give Shohenchi a lily as an offering." He turned to the chancellor of the exchequer, whose face was buried beneath a black beard. "Chancellor, go to the forest and find me a lily in bloom."

"Very well, Your Majesty."

The chancellor went off alone to the woods. The woods were all hushed and blue, and peer about as he might, he could find no lily.

The chancellor went about the wood till, hidden among the trees, he found a large house. The sun shone bright and white, and the house looked half-bright as though in a dream. Beneath a chestnut tree that stood in front of the house, a child with bare feet stood watching him, holding in his hand a lily stem bearing ten white flowers, pure white as though carved out of shell.

The chancellor went forward.

"Sell me that flower."

"All right," said the child, pursing his lips as he spoke.

"How much is it?" asked the chancellor with a smile.

"Ten pennies," said the child briskly, in a loud voice.

"Ten pennies is too much," said the chancellor, who really felt that it was too expensive.

"Five pennies," replied the child briskly again.

"Five pennies is too much," said the chancellor with a smile, really believing that it was still too expensive.

"One penny," shouted the child, his face bright red.

"I see. One penny. Then I imagine this will do, won't it?" The chancellor took off his necklace of crimson jewels.

"Fine," shouted the child joyfully as he looked at the red stones. The chancellor handed over the necklace and took the lily in his hand.

"What do you want it for, the flower?" the child asked, as though it had only just occurred to him to wonder.

"To give to Shohenchi."

"Oh, then I can't let you have it." The child flung the necklace down on the ground.

"Why not?"

"I thought of giving it to him myself."

"Did you? Then I'll give it back to you."

"No, you may have it."

"May I?" The chancellor took the flower again.

"You're a good boy. When Shohenchi arrives, come with him to the castle. I'm the chancellor of the exchequer."

"All right, I'll come," the child shouted gleefully.

The chancellor went through the woods to the bank of the river.

"A splendid lily. Truly splendid. Thank you." The king took the lily from him, then raised it reverently before his forehead.

Suddenly, they saw a golden flush rising like a rainbow into the sky on this side of the green woods beyond the river. They all prostrated themselves. And the king knelt with them on the sand.

It all happened, I feel, somewhere, sometime, some two hundred million years ago.

The Restaurant of Many Orders

Two young gentlemen dressed just like British military men, with gleaming guns on their shoulders and two dogs like great white bears at their heels, were walking in the mountains where the leaves rustled dry underfoot. They were talking as they went.

"I must say, the country round here is really awful," said one. "Not a bird or beast in sight. I'm just dying to let fly—bang! bang!—at something. Anything, so long as it moves."

"Oh, what fun it would be to let a deer or something have two or three shots smack in his yellow flank!" said the other. "I can just see him spinning round, then flopping down with a thud."

They were really very deep in the mountains. So deep, in fact, that the professional hunter who had come as their guide went astray and wandered off somewhere. Worse still, the forest was so frightening that the two dogs like white bears both got dizzy. They howled for a while, then foamed at the mouth, and died.

"Do you know, I've lost two thousand four hundred silver pieces with this dog," said one young gentleman, casually turning its eyelids back.

"*I've* lost two thousand eight hundred pieces," said the other, tilting his head ruefully on one side.

The first young gentleman went pale.

"I think I'll be getting back," he said, gazing into the other's face.

"Well, now," said the other, "I was just beginning to get cold, and hungry as well, so I think I'll be getting back, too."

"Then let's call it a day. What does it matter. On our way back we can call at yesterday's inn and buy a dozen pieces' worth of game birds to take home."

"They had hares too, didn't they? So it'll come to the same thing in the end. Well, why don't we go home, then?"

But the annoying thing was that by now they no longer had the faintest idea of the way back.

A sudden gust of wind sprang up; the grass stirred, the leaves rustled, and the trees creaked and groaned.

"I really am hungry!" said one. "I've had an awful empty feeling under my ribs for quite a while."

"So have I," said the other. "I don't feel like walking any farther."

"Oh, for something to eat!" said the first.

The pampas grass was rustling all about them as they talked.

Just then, one of them happened to look round, and what should he see standing there but a fine brick building. Over the entrance there was a notice that said, in large letters:

RESTAURANT
WILDCAT HOUSE

"Look! This is just right," said one. "The place is civilized after all! Why don't we go in?"

"Funny," said the other, "in a place like this. But I expect we shall be able to get a meal, at any rate."

"Of course we shall, silly. What do you think the sign means?"

"Why don't we go in? I'm ready to collapse with hunger."

They stepped into the entrance hall. It was very fine, being done all over in white tiles. There was a glass door, with something written on it in gold letters.

PRAY COME IN. NO ONE NEED HAVE A MOMENT'S HESITATION.

They were terribly pleased.

"Just look at that!" said one of them. "Things always turn out right in the end. Everything's been going wrong all day, but look how lucky we are now. This place is a restaurant, but they feed you for nothing!"

"I must say, it seems like it," said the other. "That's what 'no one need have a moment's hesitation' means."

They pushed open the door and went through. On the other side was a corridor. Another notice in gold letters on the back of the glass door said:

PLUMP PARTIES AND YOUNG PARTIES ESPECIALLY WELCOME.

58

They were both overjoyed at this.

"Look, we're especially welcome, it says," said one.

"Because we satisfy both conditions!" said the other.

They walked briskly along the corridor and came to another door, this time painted bright blue.

"What a strange place! I wonder why there are so many doors?"

"This is the Russian way of doing things, of course. It's always like this in cold places or in the mountains."

They were just going to open the door when they saw a notice in yellow letters above it:

WE HOPE YOU WILL APPRECIATE THAT THIS IS A RESTAURANT OF MANY ORDERS.

"Awfully popular, this place. Just fancy, in the mountains like this."

"But of course. Why, even in the capital very few of the best restaurants are on the main streets, are they?"

As they were talking, they opened the door. A notice on the other side said:

THERE ARE RATHER A LOT OF ORDERS, BUT WE HOPE YOU WILL BE PATIENT.

"Now just what would *that* mean?" said one young gentleman, screwing up his face.

"Mm—I expect it means that there are so many orders that it takes a long time before the food comes, so please forgive us. Something like that."

"I expect so. I want to get settled down in a room as soon as possible, don't you?"

"Yes, and get seated at a table."

But it was most frustrating—there was yet another door, and by the side of it hung a mirror, with a long-handled brush lying beneath it. On the door it said in red letters:

PATRONS ARE REQUESTED TO COMB THEIR HAIR AND GET THE MUD OFF THEIR BOOTS HERE.

"Very proper, too. And back in the hall just now I was thinking this was just a place for the yokels."

"This place is very strict on etiquette. I'm sure they often have very distinguished people here."

So they neatly combed their hair and got the mud off their boots.

But no sooner had they put the brush back on its shelf than it blurred and disappeared, and a sudden gust of wind moaned through the room. They huddled together in alarm and, flinging the door open, went into the next room. Both of them were feeling that unless they fortified themselves with something warm to eat very soon, almost anything might happen.

On the other side of the door there was another unexpected sign:

PLEASE LEAVE YOUR GUNS AND CARTRIDGES HERE.

Sure enough, there was a black gun rack right by the door.

"Of course," said one young gentleman. "No one ever ate with his gun."

"I must say, there must be awfully distinguished people here all the time," said the other.

They unshouldered their guns and unbuckled their belts and put them on the rack. Now there was another door, a black one, which said:

BE KIND ENOUGH TO REMOVE YOUR HATS, OVERCOATS, AND BOOTS.

"What about it—do we take them off?"

"I suppose we'd better. They really must be *very* distinguished people they've got in the back somewhere."

They hung their hats and overcoats on the hook, then took their boots off and padded on through the door. On the other side was the inscription:

PLEASE REMOVE YOUR TIEPINS, CUFF LINKS, SPECTACLES, PURSES,
AND EVERYTHING ELSE METAL, ESPECIALLY ANYTHING POINTED.

Right by the door a fine black-painted safe stood open and waiting. It even had a lock on it.

"Of course! It seems they use electricity somewhere in the cooking. So metal things are dangerous, especially pointed things. I expect that's what it means."

60

"I suppose so. I wonder if it means you pay the bill here on the way out, then?"

"It seems like it, doesn't it?"

"Yes, that must be it."

They took off their spectacles and their cuff links and so on, put everything in the safe, and clicked the lock shut.

A little further on, they came to another door, with a glass jar standing in front of it. On the door it said:

> PLEASE SPREAD CREAM FROM THE JAR ALL OVER YOUR FACE,
> HANDS, AND FEET.

"Why should they want one to put cream on?"

"Well now, it's very cold outside, you know. If it's too warm inside one gets chapped skin, so this is to prevent it. I must say, they seem to be awfully distinguished people in the back. At this rate, we may soon be on speaking terms with the aristocracy!"

They rubbed cream from the jar on their faces and then on their hands. Then they took their socks off, and rubbed it on their feet as well. Even so, there was still some left, so they both ate some surreptitiously, pretending to be rubbing it on their faces all the while.

Then they opened the door in a great hurry—only to find a notice on the other side, which said:

> DID YOU PUT ON PLENTY OF CREAM? ON YOUR EARS TOO?

There was another, smaller jar of cream here.

"Of course—I didn't do my ears. I might well have got them chapped. The proprietor of this place is really most thoughtful."

"Yes, he's got an eye for every little detail. Incidentally, I'd like something to eat, but it doesn't look very hopeful with these eternal corridors, does it?"

But the next door was already upon them, and there was written:

> THE MEAL WILL SOON BE READY. WE WON'T KEEP YOU AS MUCH
> AS FIFTEEN MINUTES. MAKE HASTE AND SHAKE SOME PERFUME OVER
> YOUR HEAD FROM THIS BOTTLE.

61

And there in front of the door stood a shining gilt perfume bottle.

They splashed perfume over their heads. Unfortunately, though, the perfume smelled dreadfully like vinegar.

"This perfume's awfully vinegary," said one young gentleman. "What's wrong with it, do you suppose?"

"They've made a mistake," the other said. "The maid must have had a cold or something and put the wrong stuff in."

They opened the door and went through. On the other side of the door was a notice in big letters that said:

> WHAT A WEARISOME LOT OF ORDERS, YOU POOR THINGS. THERE
> ARE NO MORE, SO BE GOOD ENOUGH TO TAKE SOME SALT FROM
> THE POT AND RUB IT IN WELL ALL OVER YOU.

A fine blue china salt cellar was indeed standing there, but this time both the young gentlemen were quite horrified. They turned their cream-smeared faces to look at one another.

"I don't like the look of this," said one.

"Nor do I," said the other.

"'Lots of orders' means *they're* giving *us* orders."

"Yes—and it's my idea that 'restaurant' doesn't mean a place for serving food, but a place for cooking people and serving *them*. And that m-m-means that w-w-we . . ."

But he began to shake and tremble, and tremble and shake, so that he couldn't go on.

"Then w-w-we . . . Oh *dear*!" And the other one, too, began to quake and shiver, and shiver and quake, so that he couldn't go on either.

"Let's get out!" Still shaking all over, one of the young gentlemen pushed at the door behind him. But strange to say, it refused to budge.

At the other end was another door with two big holes and a silver knife and fork carved on it. It said:

> SO NICE OF YOU TO COME. THAT WILL DO VERY NICELY INDEED.
> NOW JUST POP INSIDE, PLEASE.

What was worse, two blue eyeballs were ogling them through the keyhole.

"Oh dear!" cried one, quivering and trembling.

"Oh *dear!*" cried the other, trembling and quivering.

And they both burst into tears.

Just then, they heard voices talking furtively on the other side of the door.

"It's no good, they've realized. It doesn't look as if they're going to rub in the salt."

"What d'you expect? The way the boss put it was all wrong—'You poor things,' and the like—stupid, I call it."

"Who cares? Either way, *we* won't get as much as the bones even."

"How right you are. But if they won't come in here, it's our responsibility."

"Shall we call them? Yes, let's. Hey, gentlemen! This way, quickly. This way! The dishes are washed, and the vegetables nicely salted. All that's left is to arrange you nicely with the greens and put you on the snowy white dishes. This way now, quickly!"

The two young gentlemen were so distressed that their faces went all crumpled like pieces of waste paper. They peered at each other and shook and shivered and wept silently.

There were chuckles on the other side of the door, then a voice shouted again, "This way, this way! If you cry like that, you know, you'll wash off all the cream you put on specially. (Yes, sir, coming sir. We'll be bringing it in just a moment, sir.) Come on, this way now!"

"This way, quickly. The boss has his napkin tucked in and his knife in his hand and he's licking his lips, just waiting for you."

But the two young gentlemen just wept and wept and wept and wept.

Then, all of a sudden, they heard a "woof, woof," and a "grr!" behind them, and the two dogs like white bears came bursting through the door and into the room. The eyes behind the keyhole disappeared in a twinkling. Round and round the room the dogs rushed, snarling, then with another great "woof!" threw themselves at the next door. The door banged open, and they vanished inside as though swallowed up. From the pitch darkness beyond came a great miaowing and spitting and growling, then a rustling sound.

The room vanished in a puff of smoke, and the two young gentlemen found themselves standing in the grass, shivering and shaking in the cold. Their coats and boots, purses and tiepins were all there with them, hanging from the branches or lying among the roots of the trees. A gust of wind set the grass stirring, the leaves rustling, and the trees creaking and groaning.

The dogs came back, panting, and behind them someone called, "Gentlemen! Gentlemen!"

"Hey! Hey!" they shouted, suddenly recovering their spirits. "We're here, this way, quickly!"

The professional hunter in his straw cape came running towards them through the grass, and they really felt safe at last.

They ate the dumplings the guide had brought with him and returned to the capital, buying ten pieces' worth of game birds on their way.

But once back in the capital, and however long they soaked themselves in hot baths their faces that had gone all crumpled like waxed paper would never go back to normal again.

The dogs came back, panting, and behind them someone called, "Gentlemen! Gentlemen!"

"Hey! Hey!" they shouted, suddenly recovering their spirits. "We're here. This way, quickly!"

The professional hunter in his straw cape came rustling towards them through the grass, and they really felt safe at last.

They ate the dumplings the guide had brought with him and returned to the capital, buying ten pieces' worth of game birds on their way.

But even back in the capital, and however long they soaked themselves in hot baths, their faces that had gone all crumpled like waste paper would never go back to normal again.

General Son Ba-yu and the Three Physicians

The Three Physicians

Long ago, in La-yu the capital, there lived three brothers who were doctors. The oldest, Lin Pa, was an ordinary doctor for people. His younger brother, Lin Pu, was a doctor of horses and sheep, while Lin Po, the youngest of them all, was a doctor of trees and plants. The three brothers had built three hospitals with blue-tiled roofs. They stood in a row on the tip of a yellow cliff at the southernmost edge of the town, each with its own red or white banner fluttering in the breeze.

If you stood at the foot of the hill, you could see the patients going up it in a steady procession—priests with rashes from touching lacquer leaves, horses that were slightly lame, gardeners pulling carts bearing pots of rather wilted peonies, people with cages housing parrakeets—and then, when they reached the top, dividing into three groups, the sick people going to Dr. Lin Pa on the left, the horses and sheep and birds to Dr. Lin Pu in the center, and the people with trees and plants to Dr. Lin Po on the right.

All three of them were remarkably skilled at medicine and were men of considerable compassion, so that they were all what one might call excellent doctors. But fortune had not yet favored them; none of them so far had any official rank, nor were their names as yet known far and wide. But one day a strange thing happened that changed everything.

General Son Ba-yu, Guardian of the Northern Frontiers

That day, just as the sun was rising, the inhabitants of the town of La-yu heard, coming intermittently from the direction of the plain that stretched far away to the north, a strange sound like the twittering of a great flock of birds. At first, no one thought anything of it, and all went on sweeping out their shops or whatever they were doing. But shortly after breakfast the sounds grew gradually nearer, and it became clear that they came from real flutes and bugles. Suddenly, a stir ran

through the town. Mingled with the other instruments, the people could also hear the sound of drums of various kinds. Before long, merchants and craftsmen alike were quite unable to attend to their work any longer. First the soldiers guarding the gates closed them all tight, then lookouts were posted on the walls encircling the town, and word was sent to the palace.

By around noon on the same day the inhabitants could hear the sound of hooves and see the glint of armor, and voices were heard shouting commands. Whatever it was seemed to have completely surrounded the town.

The lookout soldiers and all the townsfolk felt their hearts hammer with fear as they peered out through the loopholes meant for firing arrows. Outside the walls to the north there lay a great armed host. A forest of bright, fluttering pennants and spears rose before their eyes. What made the scene particularly beautiful was that the soldiers were all gray and shaggy, so that they looked, almost, like a great cloud of smoke. At their head rode a general with piercing gaze, a pure white beard, and bent back, mounted on a white horse with a tail that stretched out stiff behind it like a broom. His mighty sword was held aloft in his hand, and in a loud voice he was singing this song:

> Guardian of the Northern Frontiers,
> General Son Ba-yu returns
> From the sands beyond the Great Wall.
> Would I could proclaim a mighty
> Victory, but in fact we're really
> All done in. It's cold up there.
> Thirty yellowed years ago,
> Mustering ten thousand troops, I
> Rode out proudly through this gate.
> What to find, though? Sky and sky and
> Still more sky, dry winds that raise the
> Sand where even the wild geese wither
> And come tumbling down.
> All the while I galloped onward
> Till my faithful steed was weary;
> Many a time he flopped down worn out.
> Then his eyes would fill with tears and
> Gaze far off across the sands;

And each time I'd take a little
Salt from underneath my armor,
Let him lick it to restore his
Strength. But now he's thirty-five; it
Takes him quite four hours or so
Just to go a dozen miles.
I myself, I'm seventy now—
Never thought I'd make it home but
We were lucky, for the enemy
Perished—not a sole survivor—
Of the beri-beri. It was
Dreadfully damp this summer, and a
Further reason was, they'd run too
Much across the sand while chasing
Us. In that sense, you might call it
Victory after all, perhaps.
One more thing you may consider
Worthy of your praise, I feel—
Off we went one hundred thousand,
Ninety thousand still return.
Bad luck on the men that died, but
Even staying at home, I'm sure that
Ten percent at least would die off
In the course of thirty years.
So, our dear old friends in La-yu,
Children too and siblings all—
Here we are back home at last, the
General Son Ba-yu and army
From the north. I think you might, then,
Open up the gates.

Back on the town ramparts there rose a great clamor. Some wept for joy, some rushed about waving their arms in the air, some tried to open the gates by themselves and were berated by the guards. A messenger, of course, went in haste to the royal palace, and the gates in the walls of the city opened with a mighty crash. The soldiers outside were so happy that they clung to their horses and wept.

General Son Ba-yu, Guardian of the Northern Frontiers, all gray about the face and shoulders, scowled deliberately to hide his feelings as he gently took up the reins of his horse and rode in, looking straight before him, at the head of his army, followed by the bugles and the various drums, the spears with their pennants, the copper halberds green with verdigris, and the soldiers with their quivers of white arrows on their backs. The horses stepped in time to the drums, while the knees of the white horse on which General Son rode creaked as though they, too, were keeping time. As they came the soldiers sang a martial strain:

> On the last day and the first a
> Black moon rises o'er the desert.
> On the nights of south and west winds,
> Even in winter the moon is red.
> When the wild goose flies up high, the
> Enemy flees into the distance.
> Mount your horse to chase him and the
> Snow comes pouring down.

The soldiers advanced. The mere sight, even, of ninety thousand troops was overwhelming.

> On the days it snows the sky is
> Dark all over, even at noon;
> Only the tracks of the wild geese show up
> Dim and white against the black.
> Flying frozen through the air the
> Sand pulls up the withered weeds.
> One by one the weeds uprooted
> Fly off towards the capital.

The crowds forming a solid barrier on either side of the road watched in tears.

General Son Ba-yu marched thus for some half a mile, and had just reached the town square when a fluttering of yellow banners in the distance told them that someone was coming from the direction of the palace. It could only mean one thing: the king had been told, and a messenger was coming to welcome them.

General Son reined in his horse, raised a hand loftily to his forehead, peered hard to make sure what it was, then suddenly saluted and hastily made to dismount from his horse. But he could not get off. His legs seemed to have become tightly

68

fastened to the horse's saddle, which in its turn was stuck firmly to the horse's back.

The stout-hearted general was greatly dismayed despite himself. Turning red in the face and twitching his mouth up at one side, he did his utmost to leap off his mount, but his body refused to budge. Poor general. As a result of thirty long years spent shouldering a heavy burden of duty on the nation's frontiers, in the dry air of the desert and without ever once dismounting from his horse, he had finally become one with it. What was worse, since not even grass could grow in the middle of the desert, the grass must have chosen the general instead, for his face and his hands were all covered with something strange and gray. It was growing on the soldiers, too.

In the meantime, the minister coming as royal messenger drew gradually nearer; already the great spears and pennants at the head of his party were visible.

"General, get off your horse!" said someone in the ranks. "It's the messenger from the king! General, off your horse!" Again the general flapped his arms about, but still his body would not come free.

Unfortunately the minister coming to welcome him was as shortsighted as a mole. He thought that the general was deliberately refusing to get off his horse and was waving his hands as some kind of order to his men.

"Insurrection!" cried the minister to his party. "Enough! Turn back!" He and his party wheeled their horses round and dashed off home in a cloud of yellow dust. When he saw what was happening, General Son's shoulders drooped and he heaved a sigh. For a while he just sat and stared, then swiftly he turned round and summoned to him his chief strategist.

"You—" he said, "take your armor off at once, take my sword and bow, and go to the palace as quickly as possible. Then tell them this: General Son Ba-yu, Guardian of the Northern Frontiers, spent thirty long years out there in the frontier desert without dismounting from his horse either by day or by night, and in the end his body became fastened to the saddle, and the saddle to the horse, so that it is quite impossible for him to appear before the king. Tell them with all due respect that he is going now to see the doctor, and will come to pay homage before long."

The chief strategist nodded, divested himself rapidly of armor and helmet, took General Son's sword, and dashed off for the palace.

The general turned to his men.

"The army will dismount, take off its helmets, and be seated on the ground,"

he commanded. "General Son is about to pay a brief visit to the doctor. While he is gone, stay here, still and without noise. Do you understand?"

"We understand, General!" came the simultaneous cry from all the soldiers. The general held up his hand for silence, then flicked at his horse with his whip. The celebrated white steed that so often had sunk down with fatigue on the sands of the desert summoned its last remaining strength and, with a rattling of bones, dashed off swifter than the wind. For some two miles the general urged on his horse as though in a dream, till finally he arrived at the foot of a large hill, where he suddenly demanded, "Who is the best doctor around here?"

"Why, Dr. Lin Pa," said a carpenter.

"Where does this Lin Pa live?"

"Up there on the very top of this hill. The left of those three banners is his."

"Right! Gee-up!" And with a flick of his whip on his white steed, the general galloped all the way up the hill without stopping.

The carpenter was left grumbling to himself.

"There's an uncivilized fellow!" he complained. "Asks a man for information and all he can say is 'Right, gee-up!'"

But General Son Ba-yu could not have cared less. Leaping over the doctor's patients who were standing about the place, he had already arrived before the entrance gateway. And sure enough, on the gatepost, there was a sign that said in gold letters, "Dr. Lin Pa, Physician."

Dr. Lin Pa

General Son Ba-yu rode through Dr. Lin Pa's great entrance hall and steadily advanced along the corridor. As befitted the clinic of Dr. Lin Pa, the ceilings and doors of the rooms were all about twenty feet high.

"Where's the doctor? I want him to examine me!" bawled the general imperiously.

"And who might you be?" said a pupil of the doctor's, who wore a long yellow robe and had his head shaved, as he grabbed the horse's bit. "Don't you think it's a bit high-handed to come riding in here on your horse?"

"Are you Lin Pa the doctor?" demanded the general. "If so, hurry up and examine me."

"No. Dr. Lin Pa is in the room over there. But if you want something, you'll have to get off your horse."

"That's just what I can't do. If I could get off when I wanted to, I should be in the king's presence by now."

"I see. So you can't get off your horse. You've got stiffening of the legs. Very well, then. Come along."

The student opened a door at the other end. With a clatter of hooves General Son rode in. The room was full of people, in the very center of whom a small man who looked like the doctor sat on a chair examining people's eyes.

"Here, have a look at me, will you?" said the general in a friendly way. "Can't get off my horse, you know."

Dr. Lin Pa neither moved nor looked in the general's direction, but went on examining eyes as intently as before.

"Here, you!" shouted the general without warning. "Hurry up and have a look at me!" The patients all started in alarm. But the student said in a quiet voice, "There's an order for being examined. You're the ninety-sixth, and the doctor's on the sixth patient now, so you'll have to wait another ninety."

"Silence! Are you saying I should wait for seventy-two turns? Who do you think I am? I am General Son Ba-yu, Guardian of the Northern Frontiers! I have ninety thousand troops awaiting me in the town square. If I wait one turn, then seventy-two thousand troops will be waiting here with me. If you don't take me at once I shall kick the place to pieces!"

He raised his whip, the horse reared up, and the patients began to weep. But still Dr. Lin Pa did not bat an eyelid or give the general so much as a glance. A young girl in yellow twill stood up on the doctor's left, took a flower of some kind or other from a vase and, dipping it in water, held it out gently to the horse. The horse munched it down and heaved a mighty sigh. Then suddenly it folded its four legs beneath it, gave a great snore, dropped its head, and went off to sleep. General Son was quite taken aback.

"Oh, this horse! He's let me down again. Oh dear, oh dear, oh dear!" In great haste he took out a bag of salt from under his armor and tried to make the horse eat some.

"Stop it, now! Here, wake up! After all the hard times we've had together, what do you mean by letting yourself die just when we've got back to the capital at last? Come on, now—wake up! Gee-up, giddy-up! Here, just a mouthful of this salt." But the horse stayed fast asleep. Finally, General Son burst into tears.

"Here . . ." he said, "it doesn't matter about me, but have a look at the horse, won't you? It worked for me for thirty years up on the northern frontier."

The young woman smiled without saying a word, but at this point Dr. Lin Pa suddenly turned to look at the general, and with a keen glance that seemed to take in everything, from the pit of the general's stomach to the horse's head, said in a quiet voice, "The horse will soon get better. We only made him lie down so that we could examine you. Now, did you get sick at all while you were up north?"

"No, I didn't get sick. Not sick, but sometimes I had a hard time being cheated by foxes."

"How, exactly?"

"The foxes up there are a particularly bad lot. They can put a whole army of close on ten thousand under their spell. They show lights at night, or suddenly produce a great sea in the desert in the daytime. Why, they even make walled cities sometimes. They're a really bad lot."

"The foxes do all that, do they?"

"The foxes, and sometimes the sakotsu. The sakotsu's a bird. It flies high so long as no one's around, but when it sees someone it comes to investigate. Pulls the hair out of horses' tails and things like that. Sometimes it goes for the eyes too, so whenever they know it's about the horses tremble so much they can hardly walk."

"Once you've been put under a spell, about how many days does it take to get better?"

"Let's see . . . I'd say about four days. Though sometimes it seems to take five."

"Now, how many times have you yourself been bewitched?"

"Very seldom—about ten times, perhaps."

"I'd like to ask you something, then. What do one hundred and one hundred make?"

"One hundred and eighty."

"And two hundred and two hundred?"

"Let's see . . . three hundred and sixty, if I'm not mistaken."

"Just one more, then. What's twice ten?"

"Eighteen, of course."

"I see. Yes, I see very well. Even now, you're still a bit under the influence of the desert. About ten percent, in fact. Well then, I'll set you to rights."

Dr. Lin Pa waved his hands and gave directions to his students to make preparations. They brought a large copper bowl full of medicine, together with a

72

cloth. General Son stretched out his hands and carefully took the bowl from them. Then Dr. Pa rolled up one sleeve, soaked the cloth in the medicine, squeezed it out all over the helmet, and gave the helmet a shake with both hands, whereupon it slipped off without any trouble at all. Another student brought another bowl full of a different kind of medicine, and the doctor began to douse the general all over with this second medicine. The drops were quite black, and the general said anxiously, looking up with his face turned to the doctor, "I say, I wonder if the horse is all right?"

"It won't be long now," said the doctor, splashing away as before. Gradually the drops turned brown, then a pale yellow. And by the time they had finally lost all their color, General Son's white hair shone as snowy as a polar bear's. So Dr. Lin Pa threw the cloth aside, washed his hands, and the student washed his head and face. The general gave a great shudder and sat up straight on his horse.

"How about it? You feel a lot fresher now, don't you? Incidentally, how much does it make if you add one hundred and one hundred?"

"Why, two hundred, of course, doesn't it?"

"Then what do two hundred and two hundred make?"

"Let's see . . . Four hundred. Quite positive."

"Then what's twice ten?"

"Why, twenty, of course," answered the general quite unconcernedly, as though he had entirely forgotten what he had said a little earlier.

"You're quite cured. Something was blocked up in your head, and you were ten percent out in everything."

"Come, now, I'm not interested in calculations. Couldn't care less how much ten or twenty makes. I'll leave that to the mathematicians. What I'm interested in at the moment is getting you to separate me and this horse here."

"Yes . . . Well now, it's easy enough for me to separate your legs and your clothes. In fact, they should be separated already. But to separate the trousers from the saddle and the saddle from the horse is a different matter. My brother next door sees to that kind of thing, so perhaps you'd go and see him? Besides, this horse is seriously ill, too."

"Then what about this shaggy stuff growing on my face?"

"They'll take care of that also. Anyway, I'll have a student take you there."

"All right, then, I suppose I'll be getting along there. Goodbye to you."

The same girl in a yellow dress blew once into the horse's right ear. The horse sprang up, and suddenly the general found himself much taller again. He grasped

the reins and left the house at the student's side. They cut across the garden and found themselves facing a high earthen wall with a small door in it.

"I'll get them to open the back gate," said the student, going in through the door.

"Oh no, there's no need for that. A little wall like this is nothing to my horse."

The general brought his whip down on the horse. With a gee and a giddy-up, the horse had leapt over the earthen wall and ended up standing in Dr. Lin Pu's garden next door, trampling the doctor's poppy patch out of all recognition.

Dr. Lin Pu

Together with the doctor's student, General Son was ploughing on through the poppy patch when suddenly they heard the horse's fellows neighing greetings on all sides. As they entered the large building, a full twenty horses came trotting up all round them, stamping their hooves and nodding their heads in greeting to the general's horse.

On the other side of the room Dr. Lin Pu was rubbing a white ointment on a brown horse with a crooked neck. The student who had accompanied the general went forward and whispered something briefly in the doctor's ear, whereupon Lin Pu smiled and turned to face the general. The great iron breastplate Lin Pu wore was itself almost like a piece of armor. Its purpose seemed to be to prevent him from being kicked by the horses. The general rode his own horse right up to the doctor.

"Are you Dr. Lin Pu?" he asked. "I'm General Son Ba-yu. I've a favor to ask of you."

"Yes, yes, I've heard about it. Let's see, your horse is thirty-nine, isn't he?"

"More or less . . . Yes, he must be thirty-nine."

"Indeed. I'll perform the operation immediately. You may find it a bit smoky up there on the horse, though. Are you prepared to put up with it?"

"Smoky? Why should a little smoke bother me? Why, when the wind blows in the desert you have to make the horses jump at least forty-five times a minute. If you let them stop for so much as three times, they're buried up to the head before you know it."

"Indeed. Well then, let's start. Here, Fu-shu!" The student who answered his call gave a bow and fetched a small jar. Dr. Lin Pu removed the lid, took out some brownish medicine and applied it to the horse's eyes.

74

Stoneware tile set, *Horse in a Meadow*

Then he called again, "Pu-shu!" Another student gave a bow, went into the next room, and rummaged around for a while, coming back soon with a small red rice cake on a plate. The doctor took it up in his hand and spent a while squeezing it between his fingers and smelling it, till finally he seemed to make up his mind and gave it to the horse, who gulped it down. General Son, who was tired of waiting up there on the horse's back, gave a yawn. But suddenly the white horse began to tremble and tremble, and sweat and smoke began to break out all over its body. Dr. Pu retreated as though in alarm and stood watching from a distance. The horse's teeth and bones rattled and rattled, and the smoke went on rising from it. The smoke was acrid, too. At first General Son put up with it well, but before long he had both hands to his eyes and was coughing in great spasms. After a while, the smoke gradually thinned out, but now the sweat began to pour off the horse in cascades. Dr. Pu came up to the horse, put both hands on the saddle, and shook it twice.

Quite suddenly, the saddle came clean away and the general, taken by surprise, was thrown with a thud to the floor. True general that he was, however, he was up and standing straight on his feet in a flash. What was more, the saddle and the general were also quite separate again, and the general thumped busily at his bandy legs while the horse shook its back slowly as though puzzled at the sudden loss of its burden. Next, the doctor got hold of the horse's broomlike tail and gave it a mighty tug, whereupon a great white lump of something in the shape of a tail fell with a clatter to the floor. The horse busily flourished its new tail of pure hair as though pleased to find it so light again. Then three students came together in a group and wiped the horse's body all over.

"I think that will do. Now try walking." The horse quietly started walking. This time, not a sound came from its knees, which had once creaked so horribly. Dr. Pu raised his hand to bring the horse back and bowed briefly to the general.

"Most grateful, I'm sure," said the general. "Well, then, I must be off." With brisk movements, he put on the horse's saddle and flung his leg over it while the horses round about neighed loudly in farewell. Then he rode out of the room, cleared the wall, and landed in Dr. Lin Po's chrysanthemum patch next door.

Dr. Lin Po

Now the place where Dr. Lin Po cured plants and trees was a like a natural grove. The place was filled with trees and flowers of every imaginable kind standing in

rows, all of them with large gold or silver plaques attached. General Son Ha-yn got off his horse and walked slowly through them to where Dr. Po was. The student accompanying him had gone on ahead and seemed to have told the doctor about everything, for Dr. Po stood waiting with an air of the greatest deference, holding a box of medicine and a large fan. Raising a hand, General Son pointed at his face. "Here," he said. Dr. Po got a yellow powder out of the box and scattered it all over his face and shoulders; then began to fan it busily with the fan. As he did so the whiskery stuff all over the general's face turned red and began to float away like fluff, and his face became perfectly smooth as they watched. And then, for the first time in thirty long years, the general smiled.

"Well then, I'll be off. My body feels better too," said the general in delight, and swift as a gust of wind he left the room and leaped onto his horse waiting outside, which was out of the great gates of the hospital in a flash. Running after him came his students carrying bags of medicine and fans to get rid of the grey fuzz that had grown on the faces of the soldiers.

The Guardian of the Northern Frontiers Ascends to Heaven

Swift as light General Son Ha-yn shot out through Dr. Po's entrance, like a whirlwind he passed through the Lin Fu clinic next door, and, leaving the Lin Pa hospital behind him, he galloped straight on down the hill again. Since the horse was five times faster than before, he almost immediately came in sight of his soldiers resting in the distance. The soldiers, who were still looking anxiously in the direction he had gone, gave a spontaneous cry of joy and rose to their feet as one man when they saw him; then, the chief strategist who had gone as a messenger came running from the direction of the palace, marched straight for where they were.

"The king understands completely. He was even graciously pleased to shed a tear when he heard about you, and he now awaits your arrival." Just then, the students from the hospital came with the medicine. Joyfully the troops shook the powder over themselves, and vigorously plied the fans. As a result, all ninety thousand of them at once regained their clear-cut outlines.

The general gave the command in a loud voice. "On your horses! Attention!" All stood in their steeds, and soon nothing was to be heard save the snuffling of nine horses that were fine.

"Forward march!" The drums and gongs sounded, the soldiers marched for-rows, all of them with large gold or silver plaques attached. General Son Ba-yu got off his horse and walked slowly through them to where Dr. Po was. The student accompanying him had gone on ahead and seemed to have told the doctor about everything, for Dr. Po stood waiting with an air of the greatest deference, holding a box of medicine and a large red fan. Raising a hand, General Son pointed at his face. "Here," he said. Dr. Po got a yellow powder out of the box and scattered it all over his face and shoulders, then began to fan him busily with the fan. As he did so the whiskery stuff all over the general's face turned red and began to float away like fluff, and his face became perfectly smooth as they watched. And then, for the first time in thirty long years, the general smiled.

"Well then, I'll be off. My body feels lighter too," said the general in delight, and swift as a gust of wind he left the room and leaped onto his horse waiting outside, which was out of the great gates of the hospital in a flash. Running after him came six students carrying bags of medicine and fans to get rid of the gray fuzz that had grown on the faces of the soldiers.

The Guardian of the Northern Frontiers Ascends to Heaven

Swift as light General Son Ba-yu shot out through Dr. Po's entrance, like a whirlwind he passed through the Lin Pu clinic next door, and, leaving the Lin Pa hospital behind him, he galloped straight on down the hill again. Since the horse was five times faster than before, he almost immediately came in sight of his soldiers resting in the distance. The soldiers, who were still looking anxiously in the direction he had gone, gave a spontaneous cry of joy and rose to their feet as one man when they saw him. Just then, the chief strategist who had gone as a messenger came running from the direction of the palace, making straight for where they were.

"The king understands completely. He was even graciously pleased to shed a tear when he heard about you, and he now awaits your arrival." Just then, the students from the hospital came with the medicine. Joyfully the troops shook the powder over themselves and vigorously plied the fans. As a result, all ninety thousand of them at once regained their clearcut outlines.

The general gave the command in a loud voice. "On your horses! Attenshun!" All straddled their steeds, and soon nothing was to be heard save the snuffling of two horses that were late.

"Forward march!" The drums and gongs sounded, the soldiers marched forward in solemn silence. Before long the ninety thousand troops were drawn up in a square, three hundred men by three hundred men, in the great courtyard of the palace.

Dismounting from his horse, General Son softly mounted the steps of the dais and prostrated himself on the floor. The king spoke.

"You have labored long and well," he said in a quiet voice. "Will you not remain here henceforth, a general among my generals, a living example to them of loyal service?"

With tears streaming from his eyes General Son Ba-yu, Guardian of the Northern Frontiers, replied to the king, "I am overcome by your majesty's gracious words. Indeed, I scarcely know for the moment how I may reply to them. But by now I am no more than a walking shadow, a thing of no worth whatever. All the while I was in the desert, I went with chest thrust proudly forward and searching gaze, ever fearful lest the enemy should be watching with scornful eyes. But now in your gracious presence, with your gracious words in my ears, suddenly I seem scarcely able even to see. My back is bowed. I beseech Your Majesty, grant me leave that I may return to my home in the country."

"Tell me, then, the names of five generals to take your place."

So General Son Ba-yu named four generals. And instead of the fifth, he asked that the three brothers Lin be appointed state physicians. The king promptly granted his request, so on the spot the general took off his armor and removed his helmet, and in their place he donned a garment of coarse linen. Then he went back to the village at the foot of Mount Su where he had been born and occupied himself, among other things, with sowing a little millet. Then he thinned out the millet. Before long the general gradually began to eat less and less, and in the end he only ate a single mouthful of the millet he had taken such trouble to grow, and for the rest drank large quantities of water.

Then, as autumn drew near, he ceased entirely to drink even water, and was often to be seen gazing up at the sky and hiccuping, or something equally unbecoming.

Before long, though no one knew quite when, the general disappeared from sight altogether. So everyone said that the worthy general had gone to the Paradise of Eternal Youth, and they built a small shrine to him on the summit of Mount Su and installed his white horse there as a divine steed. And they offered up candles and millet and set up hempen banners on poles.

But Dr. Lin Pa, who was a celebrated physician by now, would tell everyone

she met. "Come now, you don't think General Son Ba-yu could live on clouds alone, do you? I examined the general myself so I know. A man's lungs and his bowels are two quite different things. I'll wager that somewhere, in some forest, you'd find his remains."

And there were many people who thought, yes, that might very well be so he met, "Come now, you don't think General Son Ba-yu could live on clouds alone, do you? I examined the general myself, so I know. A man's lungs and his bowels are two quite different things. I'll wager that somewhere, in some forest, you'd find his remains."

And there were many people who thought, yes, that might very well be so.

The Ungrateful Rat

In the pitch-dark space in the ceiling of an old house there lived a rat.

One day, the rat was walking along the Underfloor Highway, peering about him as he went, when a weasel came dashing along from the other direction carrying a lot of something that looked good. When he saw the rat, he paused a moment and said in a rapid voice, "Hey, Rat! A lot of sugar balls have come through the hole in the closet at your place. Hurry and get some!"

His whiskers twitching with delight, the rat rushed straight off without so much as a thank you to the weasel. When he got to the place beneath the closet, however, he suddenly felt something pricking at his leg, and a tiny, shrill voice called, "Halt! Who goes there!"

The rat looked in astonishment and found it was an ant. The ant soldiers had already set up a multiple barricade all around the sugar balls, and were brandishing their black battle-axes. Twenty or thirty of them were busily breaking up the sugar balls and dissolving them ready to take back to their nest. The rat started quaking with fright.

"Entry forbidden!" said a sergeant-major ant in a deep, resonant voice. "Off home with you! Be off now, quickly!"

The rat spun round and dashed straight home into the space in the ceiling, where he got into his nest and stayed still for some while. But he was very much put out. Nothing could be done about the ants—they were soldiers, after all, and powerful. But that meek fraud of a weasel—it was infuriating, the rat thought, that he should have run all the way to the closet and got turned back by the sergeant-major of the ants just because of what the weasel had told him. So the rat sneaked out of his nest again and went to the weasel's place at the back of the timber shed.

When he saw the rat, the weasel, who was just grinding some corn into powder with his teeth, said, "Well? Didn't you find any sugar balls?"

"Weasel—I think you're terrible, to deceive someone weak like me."

"Deceive? Nonsense. There was some there, all right."

"Oh, it was there, but the ants had already got at it."

"Ants? Had they, now. They're mighty quick, those ants."

"The ants took the lot. You should pay compensation for deceiving someone weak like me. Yes, compensation!"

"It's not my fault. You were a bit late, that's all."

"That's nothing to do with it. You shouldn't deceive someone weak like me. I want compensation!"

"You're a fine one, aren't you—throwing people's kindness in their faces. All right. If you like, I'll give you my own sugar balls."

"Compensation! Compensation!"

"Here, take it then! Take as much as you can carry and get out of here. I'm sick of you and your namby-pamby ways. Take all you can carry and get out!"

In a fine rage, the weasel flung out the sugar balls. The rat gathered up just as much as he could carry, then bowed.

"You!" shouted the weasel still more angrily. "Get out! I don't want what you've left either. I'll give it to the maggots."

The rat dashed straight back to his nest in the ceiling, where he crunched his way through the sugar balls.

In this way, the rat gradually got himself disliked. In the end, there was no one who would have anything to do with him. So for want of anyone better, he began to associate with pillars, broken dustpans, buckets, brooms, and the like. He was especially friendly with a pillar.

One day, the pillar said to the rat, "Rat, it will soon be winter. We pillars will be creaking with the cold before long. You ought to get some good bedding together before it's too late. Luckily enough, just above my head there's a lot of bird feathers and other stuff that the sparrows brought in the spring. Why don't you fetch some down and take it home while the going's good? I may feel a bit cold round the head, but I'll manage somehow."

The rat thought it was a sensible idea, so that day, without delay, he set about carrying the bedding. Unfortunately, though, there was a steep slope on the way, and on the third journey the rat fell plump off it.

The pillar was startled. "Are you hurt, Rat? Are you hurt?" he called frantically, bending itself in the attempt to see.

After a while the rat got up, then with his face all twisted, he said, "Pillar, I'm shocked at you, letting this kind of thing happen to someone like me who's not strong."

82

The pillar, who felt terribly responsible for what had happened, apologized busily. "I'm sorry, Rat," he kept repeating. "Do forgive me!"

"It's not a matter of forgiving," said the rat, taking advantage of the situation. "If only you hadn't been so ready to give instructions, this wouldn't have happened to me. I want compensation. Come on, pay up!"

"But you know very well I can't. Please let me off."

"No, I don't like bullies, so you must pay me compensation. Come on now, pay up!"

Unable to do anything, the pillar wept bitterly. So the rat had no alternative but to return home to his nest. From that time on, the pillar was too scared to speak to the rat again.

It was one day some time after this that the dustpan gave the rat half a cake that someone had left. And it happened that the very next day the rat had an upset stomach. So, as usual, the rat demanded a full hundred times that the dustpan pay him compensation. The dustpan was so disgusted that he would have nothing more to do with the rat.

Later still, the bucket gave the rat a piece of washing soda and told him to wash his face with it each morning. The rat was very pleased and from the next morning on he used it every day for washing his face. But before long ten of his whiskers came out. So, sure enough, the rat went to the bucket and demanded a full hundred times that he be paid compensation. Unfortunately, however, the bucket had no whiskers, nor any other way of paying him back, so at a complete loss he just wept and apologized. And from then on he never said another word.

One by one, all the inhabitants of the kitchen in turn had the same trouble and learned to avoid the rat; in the end, they would turn away hastily at the mere sight of him.

There was, in fact, just one of them who had not yet had anything to do with the rat. It was a rattrap made of woven wire.

Rattraps ought, in theory, to be on the side of human beings, but this one had been feeling put out recently because of the advertisements in the papers with pictures showing a trap along with a cat, both labeled "disposable." Not that human beings had ever accorded the wire rattrap decent treatment, even before that. No, not once. And everybody avoided touching him as though he were something unclean. So the trap had less sympathy with human beings than with the rats. Most rats, even so, were too frightened to go anywhere near him. Every day he would call to them in a gentle voice, "Come on, Ratty, there's a mackerel

head for dinner tonight. I'll hold the cord down firmly while you eat it. Don't be frightened. Come on. I'm not the kind to slam the entrance down behind you. I'm fed up with human beings, just like you."

But the rat still said, "Pooh, I'm not going to fall for that one," or "Really, I see," or "I'll have to speak to my father and my sons about it sometime," and made off as though there was all the time in the world.

Then the next morning a manservant with a bright red face would come to look at the trap and would say, "Nothing in it again. The rats know, that's the trouble. They learn about it at rat school. All the same, let's try just one more day." And he would change the bait in the trap.

That night as usual the trap called, "Come on, come on, tonight there's some nice soft fishcake. You can just have the bait, it's quite safe. Hurry up, now."

The rat happened to be going past just then.

"Really? Trap," he said. "Will you really just let me have the bait?"

"Well, hallo," said the trap. "You're a new rat around here, aren't you? Yes, of course — just the bait. Here, come in and help yourself."

The rat popped inside, gobbled up the fish cake, popped out again and said, "That was very nice. Thanks."

"Wasn't it? I'm glad. Come again tomorrow night."

The next morning the servant came to look and said angrily, "Dammit! He's got away with the bait. This rat's a crafty one. Still, he went inside, that's something. There—there's a sardine for today." And he left half a sardine as bait.

The trap, hooked onto the bait, waited eagerly for the rat to come along. As soon as it was dark, the rat appeared.

"Good evening. I've come as you asked me to," he said very patronizingly.

The trap was a little annoyed, but swallowed his pride and said simply, "Here, help yourself."

The rat popped inside, chewed down the sardine, and popped out again. Then he said haughtily, "I'll come and eat it again for you tomorrow."

"Umph," replied the trap.

When the servant came to look the next morning he got angrier still. "Stir, brite! But I don't see how he can just get away with the bait every night. If you ask me, this trap here has taken a bribe from the rat."

"I did nothing of the kind! What an insult!" shouted the trap, but of course the servant could not hear him. Once again he left some bait, this time a piece of rotten fish cake, fastened to the trap.

head for dinner tonight. I'll hold the catch down firmly while you eat it. Don't be frightened. Come on, I'm not the kind to slam the entrance down behind you. I'm fed up with human beings, just like you."

But the rats all said, "Pooh, I'm not going to fall for that one," or "Really? I see . . . I'll have to speak to my father and my sons about it sometime," and made off as though there was all the time in the world.

Then the next morning a manservant with a bright red face would come to look at the trap and would say, "Nothing in it again. The rats know, that's the trouble. They learn about it at rat school. All the same, let's try just one more day." And he would change the bait in the trap.

That night as usual the trap called, "Come on, come on, tonight there's some nice soft fish cake. You can just have the bait, it's quite safe. Hurry up, now!"

The rat happened to be going past just then.

"Really, Trap?" he said. "Will you really just let me have the bait?"

"Well, hallo." said the trap, "You're a new rat around here, aren't you? Yes, of course—just the bait. Here, come in and help yourself."

The rat popped inside, gobbled up the fish cake, popped out again and said, "That was very nice. Thanks."

"Was it? I'm glad. Come again tomorrow night."

The next morning the servant came to look and said angrily, "Dammit! He's got away with the bait. This rat's a crafty one. Still, he went inside, that's something. There—there's a sardine for today." And he left half a sardine as bait.

The trap hooked onto the bait and waited eagerly for the rat to come along.

As soon as it was dark the rat appeared.

"Good evening. I've come as you asked me to," he said very patronizingly.

The trap was a little annoyed, but swallowed his pride and said simply, "Here, help yourself."

The rat popped inside, chewed down the sardine, and popped out again. Then he said haughtily, "I'll come and eat it again for you tomorrow."

"Umph," replied the trap.

When the servant came to look the next morning he got angrier still.

"Sly brute! But I don't see how he can just get away with the bait every night. If you ask me, this trap here has taken a bribe from the rat."

"I did nothing of the kind! What an insult!" shouted the trap, but of course the servant could not hear him. Once again he left some bait, this time a piece of rotten fish cake, fastened to the trap.

84

All day the trap fumed at the idea of being so unjustly suspected.

Night fell. The rat came out and said as though it was all a tremendous nuisance, "Ah me, it's not easy to come all the way here every day. And all for a fish head at the most. I've just about had enough. Still, I'm here now, so I might as well do him the favor of eating it. Good evening, Trap."

The trap was quivering so with rage that all he could get out was, "Help yourself."

The rat promptly popped inside, then saw that the fish cake was rotten and shouted, "Trap! This is going too far! This fish cake is rotten. How can you cheat a weak creature like me? I want compensation. Compensation!"

The trap was so angry that he could not stop his wire from rattling and quivering.

It was the quivering that did it.

With a snap and a swish, the catch that was fastened to the bait came free and the entrance to the trap fell shut. That really did it.

The rat went nearly mad.

"Terrible Trap! Liar! Cheat!" he cried, biting at the wire and dashing round and round in circles and stamping on the floor and shrieking and crying. It was a dreadful commotion. Even so, he hadn't the courage left this time to ask for compensation. The trap, too, what with pain and annoyance, could do nothing but rattle and shake and quiver. This went on all night until the morning.

The servant with the bright red face came to have a look and hopped for joy.

"Got him! Got him!" he cried. "Caught him at last! And a nasty looking brute he is too. Right, come on out now! Out you come, my beauty!"

The Nighthawk Star

The nighthawk was really a very ugly bird. His face had reddish brown blotches as though someone had daubed it with bean paste, and his beak was flat, and his mouth stretched right round to his ears. His legs were quite unsteady, and he could barely walk even a couple of yards.

Things were so bad that the other birds had only to look at the nighthawk's face to take a dislike to him. Even the lark, which is not a very beautiful bird, considered himself far better than the nighthawk. If he met the nighthawk as he was setting out in the early evening, he would turn his head away with his eyes closed disdainfully, as though the nighthawk was really too distasteful for words. And the smaller birds who liked to chatter were always saying downright unpleasant things about him.

"Well! Here he comes again," they would say. "Just *look* at that, my dear! Did you ever see anything like it? It's really a disgrace to us birds!"

"Quite. Why, just look at the great mouth! I'm sure he's related to the frogs."

And so it went on. If only he had been a simple hawk instead of a nighthawk, his name alone would have been enough to send those half-baked little birds into hiding, all quivering and pale-faced, hunched up amidst the leaves of the trees. In fact, though, the nighthawk was not a brother of the hawk, nor even a relation. Surprising to say, he was elder brother to the beautiful kingfisher and to the jewel of birds, the hummingbird. The whole family was quite harmless to other birds. The hummingbird ate the honey from flowers, and the kingfisher ate fish, while the nighthawk lived by catching winged insects. The nighthawk had no sharp claws or sharp beak even, so that no one, not even the weakest bird, was afraid of him.

It may seem strange, indeed, that he should have been called "hawk" at all. In fact, there were two reasons. One was that the nighthawk's wings were exceptionally strong, so that when he soared through the air he looked just like a hawk. The other was his voice, which was piercing and also reminded people of the real hawk.

This bothered the real hawk very much, of course. If he so much as caught sight of the nighthawk, he would hunch up his shoulders and call out to him threateningly to get his name changed quickly.

Then, early one evening, the hawk actually visited the nighthawk at his home.

"Hey, are you in?" he called. "Haven't you changed your name yet? What a shameless bird you are! Don't you see that our natures are completely different? See how proudly I range the blue skies, whereas you never come out at all except on dark, cloudy days, or at night. And take a look at my beak, too. You'd do well to compare it with your own!"

"I'm afraid I just can't do as you say, Hawk," the nighthawk replied. "I didn't choose my own name. It was given me by God."

"No, you're wrong. With *my* name, now, one might say it was given me by God, but yours is kind of borrowed—half from me and half from the night. Give it back!"

"But I *can't*, Hawk."

"Yes, you can! I'll tell you another name instead. Algernon. Algernon—right? Don't you think it's a nice name, now? When one changes one's name, of course, one has to have a ceremony to announce it to everybody. You understand? What you do is to go round to everybody's place wearing a sign saying Algernon round your neck, and you bow and you say, 'From now on, I shall be known as Algernon.'"

"Oh, I could never do that!"

"Yes, you could. You've got to! If you don't do it by the morning of the day after tomorrow, I'll crush you to death. Remember, now! The day after tomorrow in the morning, I'll go round to all the other birds' houses and ask whether you've been there or not. If there's a single one that says you haven't, that'll be the end of you!"

"But how can you expect me to do such a thing? I'd rather die. So you might as well kill me right now."

"Come now, think about it more carefully later. Algernon's not half a bad name really." And the hawk spread wide his great wings and flew off home to his own nest.

The nighthawk sat perfectly still with his eyes shut, thinking. "Why on earth should everybody dislike me so much? Actually, I know quite well. It's because my face looks as though it's been daubed with bean paste and my mouth is slit from ear to ear. But in fact I've never done a bad thing all my life. Why, once

I even rescued a baby white-eye that fell out of its nest, and took it back home. But the mother white-eye snatched it away from me as though she was recovering something from a thief. Then she laughed at me. And now—oh dear!—they want me to wear a sign round my neck saying Algernon! Whatever shall I do?"

Night was already drawing in about him, and the nighthawk flew out from his nest. The clouds hung low, gleaming unpleasantly, and the nighthawk nearly brushed against them as he flew noiselessly about the sky.

Suddenly, his mouth opened wide and, setting his wings back straight, he shot down through the sky like an arrow. Insect after insect disappeared down his throat. Then, before you could tell whether he had actually touched the earth or not, he had swung up and was shooting skywards again.

The clouds were gray by now, and a forest fire glowed red on the hills in the distance.

Whenever the nighthawk decided to strike, he flew so fast that he seemed to cleave the sky in two. But tonight, among the insects he caught, there was a beetle that struggled dreadfully as it went down his throat. The nighthawk forced it down at once, but a kind of shudder went down his back as he did so.

Now the clouds were all black, except in the east, where the forest fire, red and frightening, was reflected on them. The nighthawk flew up to the sky again, feeling something heavy on his stomach.

Another beetle went into the nighthawk's maw, but this one flapped about exactly as though it were scratching at his throat. The nighthawk got it down somehow, but even as he did so his heart gave a sudden lurch, and he started crying in a loud voice. Round and round and round the sky he circled, crying all the while.

"Oh dear," he said to himself, "here I am every night, killing beetles and all kinds of different insects. But now *I'm* going to be killed by Hawk, and there's only one of me. It's no wonder I feel so miserable. Oh, how wretched! I think I'll stop eating insects and starve to death. But then, I expect Hawk will kill me before that happens. No—I'll go away, far, far away into the sky before he can get me."

The flames of the forest fire were gradually spreading out like water, and the clouds were red as though they themselves were ablaze.

The nighthawk flew straight to the home of his younger brother, the king-fisher. Luckily enough, the beautiful kingfisher was still up, watching the distant forest fire.

the sky. The forest fire was gleaming red again tonight, and the nighthawk as he flew about found himself between the faint glow from the fire and the cold light of the stars above. Once more he flew round the sky, then suddenly made up his mind and started flying straight upward, towards the constellation of Orion in the western sky.

"Oh Stars!" he called as he went. "Bluish White Stars of the west! Won't you take me up with you? If need be, I'll willingly die in your fires."

But Orion was too busy singing his brave songs to pay the slightest heed to anything as insignificant as the nighthawk. Unsteadily and close to tears, the nighthawk came down until he finally reached a resting place. Once more he flew around the sky. Then off he went straight upward again, this time towards the Great Dog in the south.

"Oh Stars!" he cried as he went. "Blue Stars of the south! Won't you take me up with you? I'll gladly die in your fires if need be."

"Foolish talk!" said the Great Dog, busily winking blue and purple and yellow. "Whoever do you think you are? A mere bird—that's all. Why, to reach here with your wings would take hundreds and thousands and millions of billions of years!" And the Great Dog turned away again.

Disheartened, the nighthawk wavered back down to earth. He flew around the sky twice. Then again he summoned up his resolve and flew straight up in the direction of the Great Bear in the north.

"Oh Blue Stars of the north!" he cried as he went. "Won't you take me up with you?"

"Now, you mustn't say things you shouldn't," said the Great Bear softly. "Go and cool yourself off a little. At times like this, it's best to dive into a sea with icebergs, but if there's no sea handy, a cup of water with some ice in it will do nicely."

The nighthawk zigzagged dejectedly down to earth again. He flew around the sky four more times. Then he called out once more, to the Eagle, which had just risen on the opposite bank of the Milky Way.

"Oh White Stars of the east! Won't you take me up with you? I'll happily die in your fires if need be."

"Dear me, no. Quite out of the question!" said the Eagle pompously. "One must have the proper social status in order to become a star. And it takes a great deal of money, too."

All his remaining strength left the nighthawk. He folded in his wings and

"Good evening, Elder Brother," he said as he saw the nighthawk flying down towards him. "What brings you so unexpectedly?"

"It's just that I'm going far away, and I've come to see you before I go."

"But you mustn't, Elder Brother! Brother Hummingbird lives far away, and I shall be left all alone!"

"I'm afraid it can't be helped. Please don't say any more today. And you—please be sure not to catch any more fish than is absolutely necessary. Please. Goodbye."

"What's happened, Elder Brother? Here—don't go just yet!"

"No. It won't make any difference, however long I stay. Give Hummingbird my love when you see him. Goodbye. We shall never meet again. Goodbye."

And he went home weeping The brief summer night was already giving way to the dawn.

The leaves of the ferns swayed green and gold, drinking in the morning mist. The nighthawk cried out loud and harsh. Then he made his nest neat and tidy, combed every bit of feather and down on his body into place, and set off from his nest again.

The mist cleared, and as it did so the sun climbed from the east. It was so dazzling that the nighthawk wavered for a moment, but he persevered and flew straight ahead in the direction of the sun.

"Sun, Sun," he called. "Won't you take me up with you? I'll gladly die in your fire if need be. My body may be ugly, yet it will surely give out a tiny light as it burns. Won't you take me up with you?"

But though he flew and flew, the sun grew no closer. In fact, it seemed to grow smaller and more distant still.

"Nighthawk, eh?" said the sun. "Why yes, I suppose you do have a hard time. Why don't you fly up into the sky tonight and ask the stars instead? You're really a bird of the night, you see."

The nighthawk gave what was meant to be a bow, but suddenly lost his balance and ended by falling down, down into the grass on the plain below.

For a while, everything was a dream. It seemed to the nighthawk that he was climbing up amidst the red and yellow stars, or that he was being swept away and away by the wind, or that the hawk had come and was crushing him in his claws.

Then something cold fell on his face, and he opened his eyes. The dew was dripping from a stem of young pampas grass. It was quite dark, and the deep indigo sky was covered all over with twinkling stars. The nighthawk flew up into

plummeted down towards the earth. But then, just when his weak legs were only inches from the ground, the nighthawk quite suddenly began to shoot upwards again like a rocket. Up he went, and when he came to the middle regions of the sky, he shook his body and ruffled up his feathers just as an eagle does before it attacks a bear.

He called and called again in a harsh, piercing voice. It was the voice of a hawk, and all the other birds who were asleep on the plains and in the woods below awoke and trembled as they looked up wonderingly at the starry sky.

The nighthawk climbed straight up and up, ever farther up into the sky. Now the flames of the forest fire below were no bigger than a burning cigarette end, yet still he climbed, up and up. His breath froze white on his breast with the cold, and the air grew thinner, so that he had to move his wings more and more frantically to keep going.

Yet the stars did not change their size. The nighthawk wheezed at each breath like a pair of bellows. The cold and the frost pierced him like swords. In the end, his wings went completely numb and useless. Then, with tearful eyes, he gazed once more up into the sky—and that was the last of the nighthawk. No longer did he know whether he was falling or climbing, whether he was facing upward or downward. But his heart was at peace now, and his great, bloodied beak, though a little twisted, was surely smiling a little.

A while later, the nighthawk opened his eyes quite clearly, and saw that his own body was glowing gently with a beautiful blue light like burning phosphorus.

Next to him was Cassiopeia. The bluish white light of the Milky Way lay just at his back.

And the nighthawk star went on burning. It burned forever and forever. It is still burning to this day.

Wildcat and the Acorns

One Saturday evening, a most peculiar postcard arrived at Ichiro's house. This is what it said:

September 19

Mr. Ichiro Kaneta:
Pleased to know as how you're well. Tomorrow I've
got a difficult case to judge, so please come. Please
don't bring no firearms.

Yours respectfully,
Wildcat

That was all. The writing was terrible, and the ink so blobby it nearly stuck to the fingers. But Ichiro was beside himself with joy. He put the card in his satchel when no one was looking and took it to school, and all day long he was bouncing up and down with delight.

Even after he'd crept into bed that night, he still kept imagining Wildcat's face with its cat's grin, and the scene at tomorrow's trial, and so many other things that he couldn't sleep until quite late.

When he awoke, though, it was already broad daylight. He went outside, and there were the hills lined up beneath a bright blue sky, rising as fresh and clean as though they'd just been made. He hurried through his breakfast and set off alone up the path by the stream in the valley. There was a fresh morning breeze, and at each puff the chestnut trees showered their nuts in all directions. Ichiro looked up at them.

"Chestnut Trees, Chestnut Trees," he called. "Did Wildcat pass this way?"

And the chestnut trees paused a while in their rustling and replied, "Wildcat? Yes, he rushed past in a carriage early this morning, going to the east."

"The east? That's the direction I'm going. How strange! At any rate, I'll keep on this way and see. Thank you, Chestnut Trees."

The chestnut trees made no answer, but went on scattering their nuts in all

directions. So Jehro went a little farther, and came to the Flute Falls. They were called the Flute Falls because there was a small hole about halfway up a pure white cliff, through which the water spurted, whistling like a flute before turning into a waterfall and dropping with a roar into the valley below. Facing the waterfall, Jehro shouted up at it.

"Hello there, Flute Falls! Did Wildcat pass this way?"

"Wildcat," replied the waterfall in a high, whiny voice. "Yes, he rushed past in a carriage a while ago, going to the west."

"The west," said Jehro. "That's the way my home is. How strange! Anyway, I'll go a bit farther and see. Thank you, Waterfall."

But the waterfall was already whistling to itself as it always did. So Jehro went a little farther and came to a birch tree. Under the tree, a crowd of white mushrooms were playing together in a strange kind of orchestra, tiddley-tum-tum, tiddley-tum-tum. Jehro bent down towards them.

"Hello, Mushrooms," he said. "Did Wildcat pass this way?"

"Wildcat," replied the mushrooms. "Yes, he rushed past in a carriage early this morning, going to the south."

"That's strange," said Jehro, racking his brains. "That's in those mountains over there. Anyway, I'll go a bit farther and see. Thank you, Mushrooms."

But the mushrooms were already busy again, playing their strange music, tiddley-tum-tum, tiddley-tum-tum.

Jehro was walking on, when he noticed a squirrel hopping about in the branches of a walnut tree.

"You, Squirrel," called Jehro, beckoning to him to stop. "Did Wildcat pass this way?"

"Wildcat," said the squirrel, shading his eyes with a paw as he peered down at Jehro. "Yes, he rushed past this morning in a carriage while it was still dark, going to the south."

"The south," said Jehro. "That's strange—that's twice I've been told that. Ah well, I'll go a bit farther and see. Thank you, Squirrel."

But the squirrel had gone. All he could see was the topmost branches of the walnut tree swaying a little, and the leaves of the neighbouring birch tree flashing for a moment in the sun.

A little farther on and the path along the stream grew narrower, then disappeared altogether. There was a small new path, however, leading up towards the dark wood to the north of the stream, so Jehro set off up it. The branches of directions. So Ichiro went a little farther, and came to the Flute Falls. They were called the Flute Falls because there was a small hole about halfway up a pure white cliff, through which the water spurted, whistling like a flute before turning into a waterfall and dropping with a roar into the valley below. Facing the waterfall, Ichiro shouted up at it.

"Hello there, Flute Falls! Did Wildcat pass this way?"

"Wildcat?" replied the waterfall in a high, whistly voice. "Yes, he rushed past in a carriage a while ago, going to the west."

"The west?" said Ichiro. "That's the way my home is. How strange! Anyway, I'll go a bit farther and see. Thank you, Waterfall."

But the waterfall was already whistling to itself as it always did. So Ichiro went a little farther and came to a beech tree. Under the tree, a crowd of white mushrooms were playing together in a strange kind of orchestra, tiddley-tum-tum, tiddley-tum-tum. Ichiro bent down towards them.

"Hello, Mushrooms," he said. "Did Wildcat pass this way?"

"Wildcat?" replied the mushrooms. "Yes, he rushed past in a carriage early this morning, going to the south."

"That's strange," said Ichiro, racking his brains. "That's in those mountains over there. Anyway, I'll go a bit farther and see. Thank you, Mushrooms."

But the mushrooms were already busy again, playing their strange music, tiddley-tum-tum, tiddley-tum-tum. . . .

Ichiro was walking on, when he noticed a squirrel hopping about in the branches of a walnut tree.

"You, Squirrel!" called Ichiro, beckoning to him to stop. "Did Wildcat pass this way?"

"Wildcat?" said the squirrel, shading his eyes with a paw as he peered down at Ichiro. "Yes, he rushed past this morning in a carriage while it was still dark, going to the south."

"The south?" said Ichiro. "That's strange—that's twice I've been told that. Ah well, I'll go a bit farther and see. Thank you, Squirrel."

But the squirrel had gone. All he could see was the topmost branches of the walnut tree swaying a little, and the leaves of the neighboring beech tree flashing for a moment in the sun.

A little farther on and the path along the stream grew narrower, then disappeared altogether. There was a small new path, however, leading up towards the dark wood to the south of the stream, so Ichiro set off up it. The branches of

94

the trees were heavy and so densely growing that not the tiniest patch of blue sky was to be seen. The path became steeper and steeper. Ichiro's face turned bright red, and the sweat fell in great drops. But then, quite suddenly, he came out into the light. He had reached a beautiful golden meadow. The grass rustled in the breeze, and all around stood fine, olive-colored trees.

There, in the middle of the meadow, a most odd-looking little man was watching Ichiro. His back was bent, and in his hand he held a leather whip. Ichiro slowly went nearer to him, then stopped in astonishment. The little man was one-eyed, and his blind eye, which was white, was moving nervously all the time. His legs were very bandy, like a goat's, and—most peculiar of all—his feet were shaped like spades.

"Do you happen to know Wildcat?" Ichiro asked, trying not to show his nervousness. The little man looked at Ichiro with his one eye, and his mouth twisted into a leer.

"Mr. Wildcat will be back in just a moment," he said. "You'll be Ichiro, I suppose?"

Ichiro started back in astonishment.

"Yes, I'm Ichiro," he replied. "But how did you know?"

The strange little man gave an even broader leer.

"Then you got the postcard?" he asked.

"Yes, that's why I came," Ichiro said.

"Terribly bad style, wasn't it?" asked the little man, looking gloomily down at the ground. Ichiro felt sorry for him.

"No," he said. "It seemed very good to me."

The little man gasped for joy and blushed to the tips of his ears. He pulled his coat open at the neck to cool himself, and asked, "Was the writing very good too?"

Ichiro couldn't help smiling.

"Very good," he said. "I doubt if even a fifth grader could write that well."

The little man suddenly looked depressed again.

"When you say fifth grader, you mean at primary school, I suppose?" His voice was so listless and pathetic that Ichiro was alarmed.

"Oh, no," he said hastily. "At university."

The little man cheered up again and grinned so broadly that his face seemed to be all mouth.

"I wrote that postcard," he shouted.

"Just who are you, then?" asked Ichiro, trying not to smile.

"I am Mr. Wildcat's coachman!" he replied.

A sudden gust of wind rippled over the grass, and the coachman gave a deep bow. Puzzled, Ichiro turned round, and there was Wildcat, standing behind him. He wore a fine coat of yellow brocade, and his green eyes as he stared at Ichiro were perfectly round. Ichiro barely had time to note that his ears were pointed and stuck up just like an ordinary cat's, when Wildcat gave a stiff little bow.

"Oh, good morning," said Ichiro politely, bowing in return. "Thank you for the postcard."

"Good morning," said Wildcat, pulling his whiskers out stiff and sticking out his chest. "I'm pleased to see you. The fact is, a most troublesome dispute arose the day before yesterday, and I don't quite know how to judge it, so I thought I might ask your opinion. But anyhow, make yourself at home, won't you? The acorns should be here any moment now. Really, you know, I have a lot of trouble with this trial every year."

He took a cigarette case from inside his coat, and put a cigarette in his mouth.

"Won't you have one?" he asked, and offered the case to Ichiro.

"Oh, no thank you," said Ichiro, startled.

"Ho, ho! Of course, you're still young," said Wildcat with a lordly kind of laugh. He struck a match and, screwing up his face self-consciously, puffed out a cloud of blue smoke. His coachman, who was standing by stiffly awaiting orders, seemed to be dying for a cigarette himself, for big tears were rolling down his face.

Just then, Ichiro heard a tiny crackling sound at his feet, like salt being put on the fire. He bent down in surprise to look and saw that the ground was covered with little round gold things, all twinkling away in the grass. He looked closer and found that they were acorns—there must have been over three hundred of them—all wearing red trousers and all chattering away about something at the top of their voices.

"Here they come! Just like a lot of ants," said Wildcat, throwing away his cigarette. Hurriedly he gave orders to the coachman. "You there, ring the bell," he said. "And cut the grass just there, where it's sunny."

The coachman took a big sickle from his side and feverishly swished down the grass in front of Wildcat. Immediately, the acorns came rushing out from the grass on all sides, glittering in the sun as they came, and began to chatter and clamor.

The coachman rang his bell. Clang, clang! it went. Clang, clang! the sound

96

echoed through the woods, and the golden acorns became a little quieter. Unnoticed by Ichiro, Wildcat had put on a long black satin gown and was now sitting looking important in front of the acorns. It reminded Ichiro of pictures he had seen of crowds of tiny worshipers before a great, bronze idol.

Swish, crack! swish, crack! went the coachman with his whip. The sky was blue and cloudless, and the acorns sparkled most beautifully.

Don't you know this is the third day this case has been going on?" Wildcat began. "Now, why don't you call it off and make up with each other?"

His voice was a little worried, but he forced himself to sound important. No sooner had he spoken, however, than the acorns set up a commotion.

"No, it won't do! Whatever you say, the one with the most pointed head is best. And it's me who's the most pointed."

"No, you're wrong, the roundest one's best. I'm the roundest!"

"It's size, I tell you! The biggest. I'm the biggest, so I'm the best!"

"You're wrong there! I'm much bigger. Don't you remember the judge said so yesterday?"

"You're all wrong! It's the one who's the tallest. The tallest one, I tell you!"

"No, it's the one who's best at pushing and shoving. That's what settles it!"

The acorns were chattering so noisily that in the end one had absolutely no idea what it was all about. It was like stirring up a hornets' nest.

"That's enough," Wildcat bawled. "Where do you think you are! Silence! Silence!"

Swish, crack! went the coachman's whip, and at last the acorns were still.

"Don't you know this is the third day this trial has been going on?" demanded Wildcat, twisting his whiskers till they stood on end. "How about calling it off now and making things up?"

"No, no, it's no good. Whatever you say, the one with the most pointed head's best."

"No, you're wrong. The roundest one's best!"

"No he's not, it's the biggest!"

Chatter, chatter, chatter again, till you had no idea what it was all about.

"Enough! Where do you think you are!" Wildcat shouted. "Silence! Silence!"

Swish, crack! went the coachmen's whip again. Wildcat twisted his whiskers till they stood on end, then started again.

"Don't you know this is the third day this case has been going on? Why don't you call it off and make things up!"

"No, no, it's no good! The one with the most pointed head . . ." Chatter, chatter, chatter. . . .

"That's enough!" Wildcat shouted again. "Where do you think you are! Silence! Silence!"

Again the coachman's whip went swish, crack! and the acorns fell silent once more.

"You see what it's like," whispered Wildcat to Ichiro. "What do you think I ought to do?"

Ichiro smiled. "Well, then, how about giving a verdict like this?" he said. "Tell them that the best is the one who's most stupid, most ridiculous, and most good-for-nothing. I heard that in a sermon, you know."

Wildcat nodded wisely and prepared to give his verdict. With an enormous air of importance, he pulled open his satin gown at the neck so that the yellow brocade coat showed a little. Then he spoke.

"Right! Be quiet now! Here is my verdict. The best of you is the one who is least important, most foolish, most ridiculous, absolutely good-for-nothing, and completely crackbrained!"

A hush fell over the acorns, such a complete hush that you could have heard a pin drop.

Wildcat took off his black satin gown and, wiping the sweat from his forehead, took Ichiro's hand, while the coachman cracked his whip five or six times for sheer joy.

"I'm most obliged to you," said Wildcat to Ichiro. "I must say, you've taken a most awkward case off my hands in not so much as a minute and a half. I do hope you'll act as honorary judge for my court in future. If ever I send you a postcard from now on, please come, won't you? I'll see you're suitably rewarded every time."

"Of course I'll come," said Ichiro. "But I don't want any reward."

"Oh, no," objected Wildcat. "You must accept a reward. It's a matter of honor for me, you see. And from now on, I'll address the postcard 'Ichiro Kaneta, Esq.,' and call this 'The Court'—is that all right?"

"That's fine," said Ichiro.

Wildcat was silent for a moment, twirling his whiskers as though there was something more he wanted to say. Then he seemed to take courage and went on, "And about the wording of the card—how would it be if I put it like this: 'Pertaining to certain business in hand, your presence in court is formally requested'?"

Ichiro smiled. "It seems a little funny to me, somehow," he said. "Perhaps you'd better leave that bit out, at any rate."

Wildcat gazed crestfallen at the ground, still twiddling his whiskers as though regretting that he hadn't put it better. Finally, with a sigh, he went on, "Well, then, we'll leave it as it stands. Oh yes—about your reward for today. Which do you prefer, a pint of gold acorns or a salted salmon head?"

"The gold acorns, please," replied Ichiro.

Wildcat straightway turned to the coachman, as if relieved that it hadn't been the salmon head.

"Get a pint of gold acorns," he said, speaking fast. "If there aren't enough, you can put in some gold-plated ones. And be quick!"

The coachman began to scoop the acorns into a measure. When he had finished, he gave a shout. "Just a pint," he said.

Wildcat's brocade coat flapped in the breeze. He stretched, closed his eyes, and smothered a yawn.

"Right!" he said. "Now hurry and get the coach ready."

A carriage made of a great white mushroom appeared, drawn by a horse of a most peculiar shape and gray in color, just like a rat. Wildcat turned to Ichiro.

"Well, now we'll see you home," he said.

The got into the carriage, and the coachman put the measure full of acorns in beside them. Swish, crack! and off they went. The meadow was left behind, and trees and bushes swayed by in a bluish haze. Ichiro's eyes were fixed on his gold acorns, and Wildcat was gazing quite innocently into the distance.

But as the carriage went on, the acorns lost their glitter, and when—in no time, it seemed—the carriage came to a halt, they were just the plain, ordinary, brown kind. Wildcat's yellow brocade coat, and the coachman, and the mushroom carriage—all had vanished together, and Ichiro was left standing before his own home, the measure of acorns in his hand.

From that time on, there were no more postcards signed "Yours respectfully, Wildcat." Ichiro sometimes wonders about it. Perhaps he ought to have let Wildcat write "Your presence is formally requested" after all?

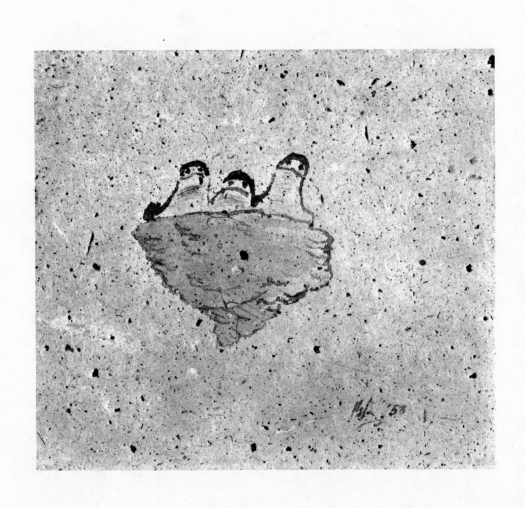

Brush drawing, *Swallows in Nest*

The Fire Stone

The hares were already in their short brown clothes.

The grasses on the stretch of open country glinted in the sun, and here and there on the birches white flowers were in bloom. The whole area was full of fragrance.

"Mm, how nice it smells," said Homoi the young hare as he hopped happily about. "Ah, how delicious! The lilies of the valley are so crisp!"

A breeze came, and the lilies of the valley tinkled as their leaves and bell-shaped flowers brushed together.

Homoi was so happy that he set off running, hop-hop, over the grass without pausing for breath. Then he stopped for a moment and, folding his front paws, panted, "It's just as though I were doing acrobatics on the water of a river."

He had, in fact, come to the bank of a small stream. The water was gurgling to itself as it ran, and the sand glittered on the bed of the stream below.

Homoi tilted his head to one side and said to himself, "Now, shall I hop across this stream? I could, perfectly easily. But somehow the grass on the other side doesn't look so good."

Just then he heard a shrill squeaking and sputtering farther up the stream, and something all darkish and bushy and shaped rather like a bird came flapping and struggling down the current.

Homoi rushed to the bank and watched intently for it to draw level with him. He was right. It was a skinny baby lark that the stream was carrying along. Without hesitating Homoi jumped into the water and grabbed tight hold of it with his front paws. But this only frightened the baby lark still more. It opened wide its yellow beak and shrieked till Homoi thought he would go deaf. Desperately, Homoi kicked at the water for all he was worth with his back legs.

"It's all right, all right!" he said, but when he looked into the lark's face he got such a shock that he very nearly let go with his paws, for the face was all crinkled, with a beak too large for it and, what was worse, a look rather like a lizard.

But the young hare was obstinate and refused to let go with his paws. His mouth was twisted with fright, but he fought it down hard and held the lark high up out of the water.

Both of them were carried steadily on. Twice Homoi's head went under the surface and he swallowed a lot of water. But still he refused to let go of the baby bird.

Then, just at a bend in the stream, he saw a small branch of a willow smacking against the surface of the water.

Homoi sank his teeth so deep into the branch that he exposed the green bark underneath. Then with all his might he threw the baby lark onto the soft grass of the bank and in a single bound leaped out himself.

The baby lark collapsed on the grass and lay shaking with the whites of its eyes showing.

Homoi was faint with tiredness, but he forced himself to go on and, pulling off a branch of white willow blossoms, covered the little bird with it. The lark raised its gray face as though to say thank you.

Homoi took one look and bounded back in horror. Then he fled, crying out at the top of his voice.

Just then something came hurtling down from the sky like an arrow. Homoi stopped and looked back. It was the mother lark. The mother lark said nothing, but clasped her child as close as possible, shaking all the while. Reassured, Homoi ran straight off back home.

Mrs. Hare, who was indoors putting together a bundle of white grass, was startled when she saw Homoi. "Heavens, is something wrong?" she said, getting the medicine chest down from a shelf. "Your face is awfully pale."

"Mother, I saved a bushy little bird from drowning," said Homoi.

"A bushy little bird?" asked his mother as she took out a dose of all-purpose powder and gave it to him. "You mean a lark?"

"I suppose so," said Homoi, taking the medicine from her. "Oh dear, my head's going round. Mother—my eyes are going funny . . ." And he flopped down on the floor. He had a terrible fever.

By the time that Homoi, thanks to his mother and father and Dr. Hare, was quite well again, the lilies of the valley were bearing small, green fruit.

One quiet, cloudless evening Homoi tried going out for the first time.

Looking up, Homoi saw something like a red star racing diagonally across the southern sky. He was watching it in wonder when, quite unexpectedly, there was a fluttering of wings and two birds came flying down out of the sky. The bigger of the two carefully placed something round and red and shining on the grass, then pressed its wings together respectfully and said, "Mr. Homoi, I and my child owe you a debt we can never repay."

Homoi took a good look at their faces by the light of the red object and asked, "Are you the larks I met the other day?"

"Yes," said the mother lark. "I must thank you sincerely for saving my son's life. We hear that you actually became ill because of what you did. I hope you are quite well by now." She bowed a great deal, then went on. "We flew around this area every day waiting for you to come out again. This is a present from our king." And placing the red, shining thing in front of Homoi, she undid a handkerchief so thin that it was like smoke. Inside was a perfectly round gem about the size of a horse chestnut, with a red flame flickering inside it.

"This is a precious stone known as the Fire Stone. The king said I was to tell you that the jewel will become still more beautiful if you look after it well. I hope you will accept it."

Homoi smiled.

"I don't need this, Mrs. Lark," he said. "Please take it with you. It's so beautiful, just to look at it is enough. I'll come and visit you when I want to see it again."

"No, I beg you to accept it," said the lark. "You see, it's a present from our king. If you don't accept it, we shall be in trouble." She turned to the baby lark. "Come boy, say goodbye. Bow properly, now. Well, we must be going."

And with two or three more bows, the mother lark and her son went off in great haste.

Homoi picked up the jewel and looked at it. Though it seemed to be burning with flickering red and yellow flames, in fact it was cold and beautifully transparent. When he put it to his eye and looked through it, there were no flames, and he could see the Milky Way as though through a piece of crystal. When he removed it from his eye, the beautiful flames flickered up again.

Holding the jewel gently in his paws, Homoi went indoors. Then he immediately went and showed it to his father. Mr. Hare took the jewel in his paw and removed his spectacles so as to examine it carefully, then he said, "This is the

famous jewel known as the Fire Stone. It's no ordinary jewel, I can tell you. They say that the only ones who ever managed to keep it properly all their lives were two birds and one fish. You'll have to take great care so that it does not lose its light."

"Don't worry, Father," said Homoi. "I'll never let that happen. The larks said the same kind of thing too. I'll breathe on it one hundred times every day and polish it one hundred times with a linnet feather."

Mrs. Hare, too, took the jewel in her paw and gazed at it for a long time. Then she said, "They say this jewel is very easily damaged. But on the other hand, when the late Minister Eagle had it there was a great volcanic eruption and the minister took it with him as he went about giving instructions for the birds to get away safely. The jewel was struck by stones and was even caught in a stream of red-hot lava, but instead of getting scratched or cloudy it actually became more beautiful than ever."

"That's right." said Mr. Hare. "It's a very celebrated story. I'm sure you'll distinguish yourself like Minister Eagle, Homoi. But you'll have to be very careful not to be unkind to others."

Suddenly, Homoi felt tired and sleepy.

"Don't worry," he said quite calmly as he lay down on his bed. "I promise you I'll be famous. Give me the stone now—I want to hold it while I sleep."

Mrs. Hare gave him the stone. He clasped it to his chest and went to sleep at once.

The dreams he had that night were so beautiful—with gold and green fires blazing in the sky, and the countryside growing all gold, and hordes of tiny windmills flying through the sky humming faintly like bees, and the Minister Eagle in all his majesty preening his glittering silver cape as he surveyed the landscape—that time and time again Homoi cried out "Hooray! Hooray!" for sheer joy.

The next morning, Homoi awoke around seven o'clock and before anything else took a look at the jewel. It was even more beautiful than the previous night.

Homoi peered into it. "I can see it! I can see it!" he exclaimed to himself. "There's the crater! There—it's erupting! Erupting! What fun, it's just like fireworks! Oh dear—the fire's pouring out of it. Now it's divided in two. It's so pretty. Fireworks, fireworks! Now it's just like lightning. There, it's started to flow! Now it's gone all gold. Hooray! There, it's erupted again!"

Mr. Hare had already gone out. Mrs. Hare came in smiling, carrying good white grass roots and green rose hips.

"Come along, now," she said. "Get your face washed and then you can try a little exercise today. Here, let me have a look. Well now, that really *is* pretty. May Mother have a look while you're washing?"

"Of course you may," said Homoi. "This jewel belongs to the family, so it's yours too, Mother." Getting up, he went and gathered six large drops of dew from the tips of the leaves of the lilies of the valley outside the entrance to their house and gave his face a thorough wash.

After he had had breakfast, Homoi breathed on the jewel a hundred times and polished it a hundred times with linnet down. Then he carefully wrapped it in linnet breast feathers, put it in the agate box that he had been keeping his telescope in, and gave it to Mrs. Hare to keep. Then he went out.

A breeze was blowing, and the dew on the grass was spilling in great drops. The bellflowers were ringing their morning chimes, "ding-dong, ding-ding-dong, ding-ding-a-dong. . . ."

Homoi hopped on till finally he halted beneath a birch tree.

Just then, an elderly wild horse came along from the opposite direction. Homoi was rather frightened and was going to turn back, but the horse bowed politely and said, "Would you be Mr. Homoi? I hear that the Fire Stone has come to you and I want to congratulate you. They say that twelve hundred years have passed since the jewel last came to the animals. Why, even your humble servant here wept this morning when he heard the news." And great tears rolled from the horse's eyes.

Homoi was dismayed, but the horse cried so much that in the end he found himself getting a little snuffly too.

"We are all indebted to you," said the horse, getting out a handkerchief the size of a small sheet and wiping away his tears. "Please take the greatest care of your health." He bowed politely again and went off in the other direction.

Homoi walked on, lost in thought, half pleased and half embarrassed at what had happened, till he came to an elderberry tree. Under the tree, two young squirrels were nibbling together at a single white rice cake, but when they saw Homoi coming they straightened up in alarm, hastily setting their collars straight and blinking their eyes as they tried to gulp down the sticky cake.

"Good morning, Squirrels," said Homoi, greeting them as usual. But the two squirrels just stood there quite rigid, unable to get a word out.

"Squirrels," said Homoi in alarm, "let's go somewhere to play again today, shall we?" But the squirrels gazed at each other with big round eyes as though the idea was quite outrageous, then suddenly whipped round and ran off as hard as they could go in the opposite direction.

Homoi was disgusted. He went home in a great state and said to Mrs. Hare, "Mother, there's something funny about the way everybody behaves. The squirrels—they won't have anything more to do with me."

"I don't imagine so, either," said Mrs. Hare with a smile. "They'll be shy because you've become so famous. So you must be careful not to do anything people might laugh at later."

"Don't worry, Mother, I won't," said Homoi. "Does that mean I'm the big general, then?"

"Well . . . yes, it does," said Mrs. Hare looking pleased.

Homoi jumped for joy.

"Hooray, hooray! They're all my soldiers now. I'll never be scared of old Fox again. Mother—I think I'll make the squirrels my major-generals. And the horse—let's see, the horse can be my colonel."

"Yes, why not?" said his mother with a smile. "But you musn't get too high-and-mighty, you know."

"Don't worry," said Homoi. "Mother, I'm going out for a while."

And without further ado, he hopped outside into the fields, where he met the wicked fox, who came dashing past directly in front of him.

Homoi trembled a little but took his courage in both hands and called, "Stop, Fox! I'm the general now, don't you know?"

"Why, dear me, yes! Would there be anything I can do for you?"

"You've always been very bad to me, haven't you? Well, from now on you're my follower."

The fox put a paw to his head as though he might well faint, and replied softly, "I really apologize most deeply. Won't you please forgive me?"

Homoi beamed with delight. "Then I'll let you off as a special favor," he said. "You can be my lieutenant. I hope you'll work well."

The fox spun round and round four times, he was so pleased.

"Thank you, thank you so much. I'll do anything you wish. Shall I go and steal a little sweet corn for you?"

"No, that would be bad. You mustn't do things like that."

"Very well, sir," said the fox scratching his head in embarrassment. "I'll never do it again. I'll await your orders in everything."

"That's right," said Homoi. "I'll call you if I want something, so don't go too far away." The fox spun round, bowed, and went off.

Homoi was beside himself with delight. He went to and fro over the open countryside, talking to himself and laughing as he thought of all kinds of pleasant things, till finally the sun sank like a broken mirror behind the distant birches, and he hurried back to his house.

Mr. Hare was already home, and that evening there were all kinds of good things to eat. That night again, Homoi had beautiful dreams.

The next day, at his mother's orders, Homoi took a winnowing basket and went out into the country where he gathered lily-of-the-valley fruit, muttering to himself as he worked, "Really! It's not right for a general to be gathering lily-of-the-valley fruit. If anyone saw me I'm sure they'd laugh at me. I wish the fox would come."

But just then he felt the ground stirring under his feet. It was a mole gradually burrowing away from him under the earth.

"Mole, Mole, master Mole," he shouted. "Do you know that I'm a great man now?"

"Is that Mr. Homoi?" said the mole in the ground. "Yes, I know very well."

"I see. That's all right, then," said Homoi very grandly. "You can be my sergeant-major. But you'll have to work a little for me."

"Why, of course. And what kind of work might it be?" asked the mole fearfully.

"I want you to gather lily-of-the-valley fruit."

"I'm terribly sorry," said the mole down in the ground, in a cold sweat of embarrassment, "but I'm just no good at doing work in the light."

"Very well, then," shouted Homoi angrily. "I won't ask you. But you just wait!"

"Please forgive me," said the mole, bowing busily. "Too much sunlight would be the death of me, you see."

"All right. All *right*," said Homoi flapping his paws irritably. "Shut up now and be off with you."

Just then, five squirrels came straggling out from under the elderberry trees. They bobbed their heads obsequiously and said, "Please, Mr. Homoi, won't you let us collect the lily-of-the-valley fruit for you?"

"Of course," said Homoi. "Go ahead. You are all my brigadiers."

The squirrels set to work, chattering with delight as they did so.

Just then, six ponies came running up and stopped in front of Homoi.

"Mr. Homoi," said the biggest of them. "Please order us to do something, too."

Homoi was delighted. "Certainly," he said. "You can all be my colonels. Be sure to come on the double whenever I call you."

The ponies jumped for joy.

"Mr. Homoi," called the mole tearfully from beneath the ground. "Won't you please order me to do something that I can manage? I promise to make a good job of it."

But Homoi was still angry. "You keep out of it," he said, stamping on the ground. "The fox'll be here soon, so I'll have him take care of you and your mates. You just see!"

Not another murmur came from the ground.

By dusk the squirrels had gathered a lot of lily-of-the-valley fruit, which they came carrying to Homoi's house amidst a great commotion.

Startled at the noise, Mrs. Hare came out of the house. "Gracious, whatever's happened, Squirrels?" she said when she saw them.

"Mother, see how skillful I am," Homoi interrupted. "There's nothing else I can't do either." Mrs. Hare thought to herself for a while, without replying.

But just then Mr. Hare came home. He stared at the scene for a while, then said, "Homoi—I wonder if you don't have a temperature. I hear you've been scaring the mole out of his life. At the mole's place they're all crying as though they've lost their senses. And who do you think is going to eat all this fruit?"

Homoi began to cry. The squirrels watched sympathetically for a while, but in the end they all crept away.

"You've done it this time," Mr. Hare went on. "Have a look at the Fire Stone. It's gone all cloudy, I'm sure."

Even Mrs. Hare was crying, and she stealthily wiped her eyes with her apron as she took the agate box containing the beautiful jewel out of the cupboard. Mr. Hare took the box from her and opened the lid, then stared in astonishment.

The jewel was blazing still redder and still more fiercely than the night before. They gazed at it in wonderment. Silently Mr. Hare handed the jewel to Homoi and started to eat. Soon Homoi's tears had dried up and, laughing happily together, they all ate their dinner and went to bed.

Early the next morning Homoi went out into the country again.

The weather was fine once more, but the lilies of the valley whose fruit had been taken were no longer tinkling as before.

The fox came running from the far side of the green grassland. He stopped in front of Homoi and said, "Mr. Homoi, I hear that you got the squirrels to gather lily-of-the-valley fruit for you yesterday. Today, how would it be if I went and found something nice for you? Something yellow and crisp—something even you, Mr. Homoi, have never seen before, if you'll excuse my saying so. And I hear you said you'd punish the mole, didn't you? He's a tricky fellow, so shall I drive him into the river?"

"No, leave the mole alone," said Homoi. "I've let him off this morning. But bring me a little of that nice food, would you?"

"Right you are!" said the fox. "I'll only keep you ten minutes. Just ten minutes!" And off he ran as swift as the wind.

So Homoi shouted in a loud voice, "Mole, Mole, master Mole! I've forgiven you now, so you don't have to cry."

Not a sound came from under the earth.

The fox came running back again across the open grassland.

"Here, try this," he said. "This is food for gods. The very best there is." And he held out a piece of rusk that he had just stolen.

Homoi took a bite and found it really very good indeed. "What tree does this grow on?" he asked the fox, who turned his face away and covered a laugh with a little cough before replying, "Why, the kitchen tree. Yes, the kitchen tree. If you like it, I'll fetch some for you every day."

"Then be sure you bring three pieces every day, won't you?" said Homoi.

"Very well, sir," said the fox, blinking his eyes to show how well he had taken it in. "But in exchange you won't stop me from catching chickens, will you?"

"Of course not," said Homoi.

"Well, then, I'll bring the other two pieces for today," said the fox and dashed off again like the wind.

Homoi's head was full of how he would take it home and give it to his father

and mother. "I'm sure even Father has never had anything as nice as this," he thought. "I'm really a very good son to them, aren't I?"

The fox came back with two pieces of bread in his mouth, placed them in front of Homoi, said goodbye in haste, and was off again immediately.

"I wonder what the fox does with himself every day," murmured Homoi to himself as he set off home.

That day, Mr. and Mrs. Hare were drying lily-of-the-valley fruit in an oven in front of their house.

"Father, I've brought something nice!" said Homoi, holding out the rusks. "Shall I give you some? Here, why don't you try it?"

Mr. Hare took it from him and removed his spectacles to have a really close look at it. Then he said, "You got this from the fox, didn't you? This has been stolen. I won't eat it." And he snatched from Homoi the piece he had ready to give his mother, threw it on the ground together with his own piece, and ground it into the earth.

Homoi burst into tears. Mrs. Hare cried with him.

"Homoi," said his father, pacing to and fro, "you're finished. Have a look at the jewel. I'm sure it's all in pieces by now."

Weeping, Mrs. Hare got out the box. Catching the light of the sun, the jewel blazed so beautifully it might have been about to ascend to heaven. Mrs. Hare handed the jewel to Homoi and fell silent. Homoi gazed at the jewel and soon forgot his tears.

The next day Homoi again went out into the country.

The fox came running up and promptly handed over three pieces of bread. Homoi hastened to put them on the shelf in the kitchen, then came out again, where he found the fox still waiting.

"Mr. Homoi, how about having some fun?"

"What kind of fun?" asked Homoi.

"How about punishing the mole?" the fox said. "He's a real plague in this part of the countryside. And he's lazy, too. If you've told him you'd let him off, I'll be a bit cruel to him myself today, and you can just stand by and watch. Why not?"

"All right. If he's a plague I don't see why we shouldn't be a bit cruel to him."

For a while the fox went to and fro sniffing at the ground and stamping at it, then finally he turned up a large stone. There, underneath, the mother, mole, and her children, all eight of them, were shivering together in a silent huddle.

and mother. "I'm sure even Father has never had anything as nice as this," he thought. "I'm really a very good son to them, aren't I?"

The fox came back with two pieces of bread in his mouth, placed them in front of Homoi, said goodbye in haste, and was off again immediately.

"I wonder what the fox does with himself every day?" murmured Homoi to himself as he set off home.

That day, Mr. and Mrs. Hare were drying lily-of-the-valley fruit in an oven in front of their house.

"Father, I've brought something nice!" said Homoi, holding out the rusks. "Shall I give you some? Here, why don't you try it?"

Mr. Hare took it from him and removed his spectacles to have a really close look at it. Then he said, "You got this from the fox, didn't you? This has been stolen. I won't eat it." And he snatched from Homoi the piece he had ready to give his mother, threw it on the ground together with his own piece, and ground it into the earth.

Homoi burst into tears. Mrs. Hare cried with him.

"Homoi," said his father, pacing to and fro, "you're finished. Have a look at the jewel. I'm sure it's all in pieces by now."

Weeping, Mrs. Hare got out the box. Catching the light of the sun, the jewel blazed so beautifully it might have been about to ascend to heaven. Mr. Hare handed the jewel to Homoi and fell silent. Homoi gazed at the jewel and soon forgot his tears.

The next day, Homoi again went out into the country.

The fox came running up and promptly handed over three pieces of bread. Homoi hastened to put them on the shelf in the kitchen, then came out again, where he found the fox still waiting.

"Mr. Homoi, how about having some fun?"

"What kind of fun?" asked Homoi.

"How about punishing the mole?" the fox said. "He's a real plague in this part of the countryside. And he's lazy, too. If you've told him you'd let him off, I'll be a bit cruel to him myself today, and you can just stand by and watch. Why not?"

"All right. If he's a plague, I don't see why we shouldn't be a bit cruel to him."

For a while the fox went to and fro sniffing at the ground and stamping at it, then finally he turned up a large stone. There, underneath, the mother mole and her children, all eight of them, were shivering together in a silent huddle.

"Come on, run!" said the fox. "Run, now, or I'll tear you to pieces!" He stamped his paw.

"Sorry, sorry!" cried the moles, trying to run away, but they were all blind and their legs refused to work. So all they did was to claw at the grass.

The smallest mole was lying on his back as though he had lost consciousness. The fox gnashed his teeth. Homoi, too, went "Shoo, shoo!" almost without thinking, and stamped on the ground.

Just then, a loud voice said, "Here, what are you up to!" and the fox spun round and round four times and shot straight off for all he was worth.

Homoi's father was standing there watching. Hastily, Mr. Hare put all the moles back in the hole and covered them with the stone again, then grabbed Homoi by the scruff of the neck and dragged him all the way back home.

His mother came out and clung to his father, weeping.

"Homoi," said Mr. Hare. "You're finished. This time, I'm sure, the Fire Stone is really in pieces. Get it out and see."

Her eyes pouring tears, Mrs. Hare went and got out the box. Mr. Hare opened the box and looked inside.

But Mr. Hare was quite astonished. The Fire Stone had never looked so beautiful. The reds and the greens and the blues were surging against each other, exploding in great bursts and showers of light; one moment lightning flashed and red light flowed like blood, then the next moment light blue flames would flare up and occupy the whole jewel, and the next moment again it would look as though it was full of red poppies and yellow tulips, of roses and masses of cherry blossoms trembling in the breeze.

Mr. Hare handed the jewel to Homoi in silence. Before long Homoi forgot his tears and was gazing happily at the jewel.

Mrs. Hare, too, stopped worrying at last and started preparing the midday meal. They all sat down and ate the rusks.

"Homoi," said his father, "You should be careful of that fox."

"Don't worry, Father," said Homoi. "What's a fox? *I've* got the Fire Stone. How could that jewel ever break or get cloudy!"

"Yes, really," said Mrs. Hare. "Such a nice jewel!"

"Do you know, Mother," said Homoi, puffing himself up proudly, "I was born to stay with the Fire Stone always. Whatever I do, do you think that jewel would fly off somewhere? And besides, I'm breathing on it and polishing it one hundred times every day."

"I only hope you're right," said his father.

That night, Homoi had a dream. He was standing on one leg on top of the summit of a tall, tall mountain pointed like an awl.

He woke up crying with fright.

❦

The next morning, Homoi went out again into the open country. Today a damp, melancholy mist was falling. Trees and small plants alike were still and silent. Even the beeches did not give so much as a flick of their leaves.

Only the morning chimes of the bellflowers rang high, high, up into the sky, "ding-dong, ding-a-dong, dong," and the last "dong" came echoing back out of the distance.

Along came the fox, wearing a pair of shorts and carrying the three rusks.

"Good morning, Fox," said Homoi.

The fox smiled an unpleasant smile.

"I got a nasty surprise yesterday," he said. "Your father's pretty stubborn, isn't he? But I expect he soon got over it. Today I've got a much better idea. Do you happen to have any objections to zoos?"

"No, not particularly," said Homoi.

The fox took a small net out of his pocket.

"Look," he said. "If you set this, you can catch dragonflies and bees and sparrows, and even jays and other bigger things. Why don't we collect them and start a zoo of our own?"

Homoi imagined to himself how a zoo would look and suddenly wanted to make one very badly.

"Yes, let's," he said. "But are you sure you can catch them with that net?"

"Oh quite sure," said the fox as though vastly amused at the question. "You go quickly, now, and leave the rusks at home. And I'll capture at least a hundred of them while you're gone."

Homoi took the rusks, hurried back home with them, put them on the kitchen shelf, then hurried back again.

The fox, he found, had got the net over a birch tree that stood there in the mist and was grinning with his mouth wide open.

"Look! I've got four already," he said, still smiling, pointing to a large glass box he must have brought from somewhere.

Sure enough, Homoi could see a jay, a nightingale, a linnet, and a siskin flapping about inside. But as soon as they recognized Homoi, they calmed down as though their fears had suddenly disappeared.

"Homoi," called the nightingale through the glass. "Please rescue us. The fox has caught us and we shall be eaten tomorrow, for sure. Please, Homoi!"

Homoi made straightaway to open the case.

But the fox frowned till dark creases formed in his forehead, and his eyes narrowed in anger.

"Homoi!" he shouted. "Watch out! Touch that case, and I'll tear you to pieces. You thief!" His mouth twisted up with rage.

Homoi felt so scared that he ran straight back home. Today Mrs. Hare was out in the fields and there was no one in the house.

Homoi's heart was beating so hard that he got out the box containing the Fire Stone and opened the lid to have a look at it.

It was still blazing brightly. But could it be his imagination, or did he see on it a tiny cloudy speck as though it had been pricked with a needle?

The speck bothered Homoi a great deal, so he huffed on the jewel as he always did, and rubbed at it lightly with a linnet's breast feather.

But the speck refused to come off. Just then, Mr. Hare came home. He soon noticed from Homoi's face that there was something wrong and said, "What's up, Homoi? Has the Fire Stone gone cloudy? You're looking terribly pale. Here—show me." He held the gem up to the light, then laughed.

"Well, what a fuss! We'll soon get this off. Why, the yellow flames are burning almost brighter than ever. Give me some linnet feathers." And Mr. Hare began busily polishing the stone. But instead of coming off, the cloudy patch seemed to get steadily bigger.

Mrs. Hare came home. Without saying anything, she took the stone from Mr. Hare and held it up to the light, then she gave a sigh and, breathing on the jewel, began rubbing at it herself.

They all took turns at polishing it with all their might, saying not a word but sighing busily all the while.

Dusk began to fall. All of a sudden, Mr. Hare stood up as though he'd suddenly remembered something.

"Well, let's have dinner shall we? You'd better try leaving it to soak in oil tonight. They say that's the best thing."

"Gracious!" said Mrs. Hare, startled. "I'd forgotten about dinner. I haven't

made anything at all. Shall we just have the lily-of-the-valley fruit from the day before yesterday and this morning's rusks?"

Mr. Hare grunted. "That'll do," he said. Heaving a sigh, Homoi put the stone in its box and stood staring at it for a long time.

They ate their dinner in silence.

"Here, I'll get the oil out for you," said Mr. Hare, getting down a bottle of nut oil from the shelf. Homoi took it and poured it into the box containing the Fire Stone. Then they put out the light and went to bed early.

Homoi woke up in the night.

Fearfully, he sat up and took a stealthy look at the Fire Stone by his bed. The Fire Stone was gleaming silver, like a fish's eye, in the oil. There were no red flames.

Homoi burst out crying.

Mr. and Mrs. Hare got up, startled, and lit the lamp.

The Fire Stone was just like a ball of lead. Weeping, Homoi told his father about the fox and his net.

In terrible dismay, Mr. Hare began hastily to get dressed, saying as he did so, "Homoi, you're a fool. I've been stupid, too. You were given the Fire Stone because you saved the baby lark's life, weren't you? But in spite of that the day before yesterday you were talking about it being yours by birth. Come on, let's go to the fields. The fox may still have his net up there. You've got to fight him, even if it kills you. I'll help you, of course."

Still weeping, Homoi stood up and went with his father. Mrs. Hare followed after them, also weeping.

The mist was falling in great clammy drops, and dawn was beginning to break. The fox was beneath the birch tree with his net still over it. And when he saw the three of them, his mouth twisted in a great sneer.

"Fox!" shouted Homoi's father. "Clever aren't you, tricking Homoi like that. Come here and fight!"

"Pooh! I could easily finish off all three of you with my teeth," the fox said with a really villainous expression, "but I don't fancy getting myself hurt. I've got other, better things to eat."

He heaved the glass box onto his shoulder and made to flee.

"No you don't!" said Homoi's father, and put a paw on the glass case. The fox staggered and in the end ran off leaving the box behind.

The case was full of a hundred or so birds, all of them weeping. Not only sparrows and jays and nightingales, but a great owl too, and even the mother lark and her son.

Homoi's father lifted the lid.

The birds all flew out and, bowing to the ground, said in chorus, "Thank you very much. We're obliged to you once again."

"Not at all," replied Homoi's father. "We are scarcely able to face you. We've made the jewel that your king gave us go cloudy."

"Why, whatever can have happened?" the birds said in chorus. "Won't you let us take a look at it?"

"Come along, then," said Homoi's father, leading the way towards the house. The birds crowded after him. Homoi followed in the rear, crestfallen and weeping. The owl walked with great, slow strides, glancing back at Homoi every now and then with a stern expression.

They all went indoors.

The birds took up every inch of space in the house—the floor, the shelves, and even the table. The owl turned his eyes in the most outrageous directions, harrumphing busily to himself all the while.

Mr. Hare picked up the jewel, which looked like nothing more than a white stone by now.

"You see! So go on, laugh at us as much as you please," he said, and at that instant the Fire Stone split in two with a sharp crack. The next moment, there was a fierce crackling, and before their gaze the stone crumbled up into a smoke-like powder.

Homoi in the doorway gave a sharp cry and fell. The powder had got into his eyes. Startled, they were moving towards him when this time there was a sputtering sound and the cloud of smoke began gradually to condense again, till it formed a number of solid pieces. Then those pieces in turn resolved themselves into only two pieces, which finally fitted together with a smart crack and once more became the Fire Stone, just as it had always been. The jewel blazed like the fires of a volcano, it shone like the sunset; and with a swishing sound it flew up, out through the window, and away.

The birds lost interest and began to leave, first one then another, till in the end only the owl was left. The owl peered about the room. "Only six days!

117

Woo-hoo," he said mockingly. "Only six days, woo-hoo!" And with a shrug of his shoulders he strode out.

What was worse, Homoi's eyes had gone white and cloudy just as the stone had done, and he could see nothing at all.

Mrs. Hare had been crying steadily from start to finish. Mr. Hare stood for a while with his arms folded, thinking. Then he patted Homoi gently on the shoulder, and said, "Don't cry. This kind of thing could happen to anybody. You're luckier than the rest, because you know now. Your eyes will get better, I'm sure. I'll see that they do. So come now, don't cry!"

Beyond the window the mist had cleared, the leaves of the lilies of the valley were glittering in the sunlight, and the bellflowers went "ding, ding, dong, ding-a, ding-a-dong," as they tolled clear and loud their morning carillon.

Night of the Festival

It was the night of the festival of the mountain god.

Wearing his new light blue sash and armed with fifteen pennies that his mother had given him for pocket money, Ryoji set off for the place where the holy palanquin had been installed. One of the sideshows set up nearby was called "The Air Beast" and was doing a roaring trade, he had heard.

A man wearing baggy trousers, with long hair and a pockmarked face, was standing in front of the curtain of the booth. Come one, come all!" he boomed. "Come and see the show!" As Ryoji strolled up to have a look at the placard, the man suddenly called out to him.

"Hey, youngster, come on in!" he called. "You can pay on the way out." Almost without thinking, Ryoji darted in through the entrance. Inside the booth, he found Kosuke and quite a number of other people he knew, all staring with half-amused, half-serious expressions at something displayed on a platform in the center.

Clinging to the top of the stand was the air beast. It was big and flattish and wobbly and white, with no particular head or mouth. When the showman poked it with a stick, it gave way on this side and swelled out on the other side, and when he poked it on the other side it came out on this side, and when he poked it in the center it swelled out all round. Ryoji felt it was stupid and was getting out as quickly as he could when his wooden clog caught in a hole in the bare earth. He nearly fell over and collided heavily with the tall, solid-looking man next to him. Looking up startled, he found it was a man with a red, heavy-boned face, wearing an old white-striped summer kimono and a peculiar garment resembling a shaggy straw cape over his shoulders. The man was looking down at him just as startled. His eyes were perfectly round and a kind of smoky gold in color.

Ryoji was still staring at him in surprise, when all of a sudden the man blinked his eyes rapidly, turned away, and made in a hurry for the exit. Ryoji went after him. At the entrance, the man opened his large right hand, which had been tightly

clenched, and produced a tenpenny silver coin. Ryoji took out a similar coin, gave it to the man at the entrance, and went outside, only to bump into his cousin Tatsuji. The man's broad shoulders disappeared into the crowd.

"Did you go into that show?" asked Tatsuji, pointing at the placard for the show. "They call it an air beast, but people say it's really only a cow's stomach full of air. I think you're stupid to pay to see something like that."

Ryoji just stared vaguely at the placard with its oddly shaped air beast. So Tatsuji went on, "I haven't been to see the holy palanquin yet. See you tomorrow." And hopping on one leg he went off into the crowd.

Ryoji, too, moved away in a hurry. The vegetables and grapes piled on the rows of stalls that lined both sides gleamed in the light of the gas lamps.

Ryoji walked on between them, thinking to himself idly that the blue flames of the gas were pretty but gave off an unpleasant smell, like that of a big snake.

Over there in the booth built for the festival dance, five paper lanterns were shedding a dim light. It seemed that the dance was about to begin, for a small cymbal was sounding quietly. Ryoji stood there idly for a while, remembering that his friend Shoichi was going to appear in the dance.

Just then he suddenly heard loud voices from the direction of the refreshment stall that stood in the dark shadow of some cypress trees, and everybody started running in that direction. Ryoji hurried over with the rest and peered round the side of the grown-ups.

The big man he had seen a while ago was standing there, his hair all unkempt, being tormented by the young men of the village. The sweat was running down his forehead as he bowed to them again and again. He was trying to say something, but stuttered so badly that he could not get the words out.

A young man of the village with a neat parting in his sleek hair was gradually shouting louder and louder because of the people watching.

"We're not going to be made fools of by an outsider like you. Pay up quickly, now! Come on, pay up! No money, eh? Why, you—! Then why did you eat sem? Eh?"

The man was in a terrible state and barely managed to get out through his stutters, "I'll b-b-b-bring you a hundred bundles of firewood."

The young man, who was proprietor of the tea booth, seemed to be rather hard of hearing, for he cried in a louder voice still, "What! Only a couple of dumplings, you say? What do you expect? I'd let you have a couple of dumplings, but I don't like your way of talking. Yes, you!"

120

Wiping away the sweat, the man just managed again to get out, "I'll bring you a hundred bundles of firewood, so let me go."

"Why, you miserable liar! Who'd pay a hundred bundles of firewood for two dumplings! Where're you from, anyway?"

"Th-th-th-th-that's something I just can't tell you. Let me go now." The man was blinking his golden eyes and wiping furiously at the sweat. He seemed to be wiping away some tears too.

"Beat him up! Beat him up!" someone shouted.

Suddenly Ryoji understood everything.

"I know," he thought, "he got terribly hungry, and he'd paid to see the air beast, then he went and ate the dumplings and forgot he hadn't got any money left. He's crying. He's not a bad man. Just the opposite—he's too honest. Right. I'll go to the rescue."

Stealthily he took from his purse the one remaining coin, grasped it tightly in his hand, and pushing his way through the crowd as unobtrusively as possible went up to the man. The man was hanging his head, with his hands resting humbly on his knees, furiously mumbling something unintelligible.

Ryoji crouched down and, without saying anything, placed the coin on top of the man's big foot in its straw sandal.

The man gave a start and stared down into Ryoji's face, then the next moment he swiftly bent down, took up the coin and straightway slammed it down on the desk in front of the proprietor, shouting in a loud voice, "There, there's your money! Now let me go. I'll bring the hundred bundles of firewood later. And four bushels of chestnuts." No sooner had he said it than he thrust the young man and the others aside and fled outside like the wind.

"It's a wild man. A wild man of the hills!" they all cried and ran after him, chattering at each other excitedly, but he had already disappeared without trace.

The wind suddenly howled, the great black cedars swayed, the bamboo curtains on the tea shop flew up, and lights blew out here and there.

Just then the flute began to play for the festival dance, but instead of going to watch it Ryoji hurried home along the dim white paths between the paddy fields. He was in a hurry to tell his grandfather about the wild man of the hills. Already the Pleiades was shining dimly quite high up in the sky.

Back at home he went in past the stable and found his grandfather all alone, cooking soybeans over a fire in the open hearth. Ryoji went quickly to sit opposite him and told him everything that had happened. At first his grandfather sat

quietly, watching Ryoji's face as he talked, but when he got to the end he burst out laughing.

"Oh yes," he laughed, "that's a wild man of the hills, all right. The wild men are very honest. I've met them in the hills myself sometimes on misty days. But I'm sure no one's ever heard of a wild man coming to see a festival before." He laughed again. "Or perhaps they've come before and nobody's noticed, eh?"

"Grandpa, what do the wild men of the hills do there?"

"Well, they say they make fox traps, for one thing, using the branches of trees. They bend down a tree as thick as this and hold it down with another branch, then they dangle down a fish or something from the end so that when a fox or bear comes to eat it, the branch springs up again and kills it."

Just then there was a great thud and rattling outside, and the whole house shook as in a earthquake. Ryoji clung tight to Grandfather. Grandfather, who had gone rather pale himself, hurried outside with a lamp.

Ryoji followed after him. The lamp blew out almost immediately, but it didn't matter, for the eighteenth-day moon was rising silently over the dark hills to the east.

And there, in the open space in front of the house, a great pile of thick faggots lay flung down on the ground. They were massive faggots, roughly broken, with thick roots and branches still attached to them. Grandfather gazed at them for a while in astonishment, then suddenly clapped his hands together and laughed. "The wild man of the hills has brought you some firewood. And there I was thinking the was going to give it to the man at the dumpling stall. The wild man's no fool."

Ryoji was stepping forward to get a better look at the firewood when suddenly he slipped on something and fell over. Looking closer, he found the whole ground was covered with bright, shiny chestnuts.

"Grandpa!" he shouted, getting up again. "The man of the hills brought chestnuts too!"

"Well! So he even brought chestnuts!" said Grandfather in astonishment. "We can't possibly accept all this. Next time I go into the hills I'll take something and leave it for him. I expect he'd like something to wear best of all."

Suddenly Ryoji had a funny feeling, as though he was sorry for the man of the hills and wanted to cry.

"Grandpa, I feel sorry for the wild man of the hills. He's too honest, isn't he? I'd like to give him something nice.

quietly, watching Ryoji's face as he talked, but when he got to the end he burst out laughing.

"Oh yes," he laughed, "that's a wild man of the hills, all right. The wild men are very honest. I've met them in the hills myself sometimes on misty days. But I'm sure no one's ever heard of a wild man coming to see a festival before." He laughed again. "Or perhaps they've come before and nobody's noticed, eh?"

"Grandpa, what do the wild men of the hills do there?"

"Well, they say they make fox traps, for one thing, using the branches of trees. They bend down a tree as thick as this and hold it down with another branch, then they dangle down a fish or something from the end so that when a fox or bear comes to eat it, the branch springs up again and kills it."

Just then there was a great thud and rattling outside, and the whole house shook as in a earthquake. Ryoji clung tight to Grandfather. Grandfather, who had gone rather pale himself, hurried outside with a lamp.

Ryoji followed after him. The lamp blew out almost immediately, but it didn't matter, for the eighteenth-day moon was rising silently over the dark hills to the east.

And there, in the open space in front of the house, a great pile of thick faggots lay flung down on the ground. They were massive faggots, roughly broken, with thick roots and branches still attached to them. Grandfather gazed at them for a while in astonishment, then suddenly clapped his hands together and laughed.

"The wild man of the hills has brought you some firewood. And there I was thinking he was going to give it to the man at the dumpling stall. The wild man's no fool!"

Ryoji was stepping forward to get a better look at the firewood when suddenly he slipped on something and fell over. Looking closer, he found the whole ground was covered with bright, shiny chestnuts.

"Grandpa!" he shouted, getting up again. "The man of the hills brought chestnuts too!"

"Well! So he even brought chestnuts!" said Grandfather in astonishment. "We can't possibly accept all this. Next time I go into the hills I'll take something and leave it for him. I expect he'd like something to wear best of all."

Suddenly Ryoji had a funny feeling, as though he was sorry for the man of the hills and wanted to cry.

"Grandpa, I feel sorry for the wild man of the hills. He's too honest, isn't he? I'd like to give him something nice."

"Yes. Next time, perhaps, I'll take him a quilted coat. A wild man might like to wear a thick, quilted coat instead of a thin, padded one for the winter. And I'll take him some dumplings."

"But that's not enough—just clothes and dumplings!" shouted Ryoji. "I want to give him something that'll make him cry and dance about the place for joy, something so nice he'll feel he's in heaven."

Grandfather picked up the extinguished lamp.

"Mm. That's if we can find such a thing," he said. "Come on, then, let's go indoors and have the beans. Your father'll be back from next door before long." And he led the way indoors.

Ryoji said nothing but looked up at the pale blue, lopsided moon.

The wind was roaring in the hills.

Etching, *Hakone*

The First Deer Dance

From a gap in the ragged, gleaming clouds to the west, the setting sun slanted down red on the mossy plain, and the swaying fronds of pampas grass shone like white fire. I was tired, and lay down to sleep. Gradually, the rustling of the breeze began to sound to my ears like human speech, and before long it was telling me the true meaning of the Deer Dance that the countryfolk still dance in the hills and on the plain of Kitakami.

Long ago, in the days when the area was still covered all over with tall grass and black forests, Kaju, together with his grandfather and the others, came to live there from somewhere east of the river Kitakami. They settled there, cleared the land, and began growing millet.

One day, Kaju fell out of a chestnut tree and hurt his knee a little. At such times, it was the local custom to go to the mountains to the west, where there was a hot spring, build a hut there, and bathe in the spring until one was cured.

One fine morning, then, Kaju set out for the spring. With his rice, his bean paste, and his pot on his back, he walked slowly, limping slightly as he went, across the open country where the plumes of pampas grass were blowing silver.

On he went, over streams and across stony wastes, till the mountain range loomed large and clear and he could pick out each single tree on the mountains like the pins on a pincushion. By now the sun was far gone in the west and glittered with a greenish tinge just above the tops of a stand of a dozen alder trees.

Kaju set the load from his back down on the grass, took out some horse-chestnut and millet dumplings, and began to eat. The pampas grass spread away from him in clump after clump—so many clumps that it seemed to ripple in shining white waves all over the plain. As he ate his dumplings, Kaju thought to himself what a fine sight the trunks of the alder trees made, rising perfectly straight out of the pampas grass.

But he had walked so energetically that he was almost too tired to eat. He was soon full, and in the end, despite himself, he had to leave a piece of dumpling about the size of a horse-chestnut burr.

"I'll leave 'er for the deer," he said to himself. "Deer do love scent and earth." And he set it down by a small white flower that grew at his feet. Then he shouldered his pack once more and slowly, quite slowly, set off again.

But he had only gone a short way when he realized that he had left his cotton towel at the place where he had rested, so he turned back again in a hurry. He could still see the stand of alder trees quite clearly, so to go back was really not much trouble. Yet before he reached the place, he suddenly stopped quite still, seeing beyond all doubt that the deer were already there.

And there, indeed, they were—at least five or six, walking towards something, with their moist noses stretched out far in front of them. Kaju tiptoed softly over the moss towards them, taking care not to brush against the pampas grass.

No mistake about it, the deer had come for the dumpling he had left. "Hah, deer can't wait to eat me," he murmured to himself with a smile and, bending down low, crept slowly in their direction.

He peeped out from behind a clump of pampas grass, then drew back in surprise. Six deer were walking round and round in a ring on the stretch of grassy turf. Hardly daring to breathe, Kaju peered out again from between the pampas grass.

The sun had reached the summit of one of the alder trees, and its topmost branches shone with a strange green light, so that it looked for all the world like some green living creature standing stock-still, gazing down at the deer. Each plume of pampas grass shone sparse and silver, and the deer's coats seemed even shinier and sleeker than usual. Delighted, Kaju gently lowered himself onto one knee and concentrated on watching the deer.

They were going round and round in a wide circle, and he soon noticed that every one of them seemed intent on something that lay in the center of the ring. He was sure of it because their heads and ears and their eyes were all pointing in that direction. What was more, from time to time one or other of them would break the circle and stagger a few paces inwards as though drawn towards the center.

In the center of the ring, of course, was the bone-chestnut dumpling that Kaju had left there a while ago. The thing that was bothering the deer so much, though, was not the dumpling itself round, but Kaju's white cotton towel, which lay in a curve where it had fallen on the ground. Bending his bad leg gently with one hand, Kaju sat himself neatly on his heels on the moss in order to watch.

Gradually the deer's circling slowed down. Now they trotted gently, every

"I'll leave 'er for the deer," he said to himself. "Deer, do 'ee come and eat!" And he set it down by a small white flower that grew at his feet. Then he shouldered his pack once more and slowly, quite slowly, set off again.

But he had only gone a short way when he realized that he had left his cotton towel at the place where he had rested, so he turned back again in a hurry. He could still see the stand of alder trees quite clearly, so to go back was really not much trouble. Yet before he reached the place, he suddenly stopped quite still, sensing beyond all doubt that the deer were already there.

And there, indeed, they were—at least five or six, walking towards something, with their moist noses stretched out far in front of them. Kaju tiptoed softly over the moss towards them, taking care not to brush against the pampas grass.

No mistake about it, the deer had come for the dumpling he had left. "Hah, deer bain't wasting no time," he muttered to himself with a smile and, bending down low, crept slowly in their direction.

He peeped out from behind a clump of pampas grass, then drew back in surprise. Six deer were walking round and round in a ring on the stretch of grassy turf. Hardly daring to breathe, Kaju peered out at them from between the pampas stems.

The sun had touched the summit of one of the alder trees, and its topmost branches shone with a strange green light, so that it looked for all the world like some green living creature standing stock still, gazing down at the deer. Each plume of pampas grass shone separate and silver, and the deer's coats seemed even shinier and sleeker than usual. Delighted, Kaju gently lowered himself onto one knee and concentrated on watching the deer.

They were going round and round in a wide circle, and he soon noticed that every one of them seemed intent on something that lay in the center of the ring. He was sure of it, because their heads and ears and their eyes were all pointing in that direction. What was more, from time to time one or the other of them would break the circle and stagger a few paces inwards as though drawn towards the center.

In the center of the ring, of course, was the horse-chestnut dumpling that Kaju had left there a while ago. The thing that was bothering the deer so much, though, was not the dumpling, it seemed, but Kaju's white cotton towel, which lay in a curve where it had fallen on the ground. Bending his bad leg gently with one hand, Kaju sat himself neatly on his heels on the moss in order to watch.

Gradually the deer's circling slowed down. Now they trotted gently, every so often breaking out of the ring and putting one foreleg forward towards the center as though about to break into a run, then just as soon drawing back again and trotting on once more. Their hooves thudded pleasantly on the dark soil of the plain. Finally, they stopped going round and round altogether and came and stood in a group between Kaju and the towel.

Without warning, Kaju's ears began to ring and his body began to shake: the same feeling that the deer were feeling, a feeling as of grass swaying in the breeze, was coming to him in waves. The next moment, he really doubted his own ears, for now he could actually hear the deer talking.

"Shall I go for to look, then?" one was saying.

"Naw, 'er be dangerous. Better watch 'er a bit longer."

"Can't get caught with no trick like old Fox played on us. 'Er be only a dumpling, when all's said and done."

"Right, right. Only too right."

So went the deer's talk.

"'Er may be alive."

"Aye, 'er be summat like a living crittur, indeed."

In the end one of them seemed to make up his mind. He straightened his back, left the ring, and went in towards the center. All the other deer stopped to watch.

The deer who had gone forward edged towards the towel inch by inch with his neck stretched out just as far as it would go and his legs all bunched up beneath him. Then, quite suddenly, he shot up in the air and came darting back like an arrow. The other five deer scattered in all four directions, but the first deer stopped dead when he got back to where he had started, so they calmed down and, reluctantly returning, gathered in front of him.

"How were it? What do 'er be? That long white thing?"

"'Er do have wrinkles all the way down 'er."

"Then 'er bain't a living crittur. 'Er be a toadstool or something after all! Poisonous too, I don't doubt."

"Naw, 'er bain't no toadstool. 'Er be a living thing all right."

"Be 'er, now! Alive and lots of wrinkles too—'er be getting on in years, then."

"Aye, that sentry guarding the dumpling be a very *elderly* sentry. Oh, ho, ho, ho, ho!"

"Eh, he, he, he, he! A blue and white sentry!"

"Oh, ho, ho, ho, ho! Private Blue-'n-White."

"Shall I go for to look now?"

"Pa'ce go now. Er be safe enough."

"Er won't bite now?"

"Naw, er be safe, I'd say."

So another deer crept slowly forward. The five who stayed behind nodded their heads approvingly, as they watched.

The deer who had gone forward seemed scared to death. Time and time again he hunched his four legs up and arched his back ready for flight, only to stretch them out again slowly and creep forward again the next moment.

At last he reached a spot only a step away from the rowel. He stretched his neck out as far as it would go and went stiff... at the rowel, then suddenly leaped up in the air, and came running back. They all started and began to run off, but the first deer stopped ahead as soon as he got back, so they took courage and gathered their faces close about the rowel.

"How were er? Why did er run away?"

"But I thought er were going to bite it."

"What can er be, now?"

"No telling. What be sure is that er be white and blue, in patches, like."

"How do er smell? Do it smell?"

"Er do smell like willow leaves."

"Do, er be, hey?"

"Now, I didn't rightly notice that."

"Shall I go now?"

"Aye, do 'ee go now.

The third deer crept slowly forward. Just then a slight breeze stirred the rowel. He halted in his tracks in fright, and the others gave a violent start. After a while, though, he seemed to calm down, and crept forward again until at last he could stretch the tip of his nose out to the rowel.

The five deer left behind were nodding at each other knowingly. But just then the deer out in front went quite still, shot up in the air, and came racing back.

"What did 'ee run away for?"

"Because I had a strange feeling, like."

"Be er breathing?"

"Well, I don't rightly think I heard er breathing. Er don't seem to have no mouth, either.

"Shall I go for to look now?"

"Do 'ee go, now. 'Er be safe enough."

" 'Er won't bite, now?"

"Naw, 'er be safe, I'd say."

So another deer crept slowly forward. The five who stayed behind nodded their heads approvingly as they watched.

The deer who had gone forward seemed scared to death. Time and time again he bunched his four legs up and arched his back ready for flight, only to stretch them out gingerly and creep forward again the next moment.

At last he reached a spot only a step away from the towel. He stretched his neck out just as far as it would go and went sniff, sniff, at the towel, then suddenly leaped up in the air and came running back. They all started and began to run off, but the first deer stopped dead as soon as he got back, so they took courage and gathered their faces close about his head.

"How were 'er? Why did 'ee run away?"

"But I thought 'er were going to bite I!"

"What *can* 'er be, now?"

"No telling. What be sure is that 'er be white and blue, in patches, like."

"How do 'er smell? Eh, the smell?"

" 'Er do smell like willow leaves."

"Do 'er breathe?"

"Now, I didn't rightly notice that."

"Shall I go now?"

"Aye, do 'ee go now."

The third deer crept slowly forward. Just then a slight breeze stirred the towel. He halted in his tracks in fright, and the others gave a violent start. After a while, though, he seemed to calm down, and crept forward again until at last he could stretch the tip of his nose out to the towel.

The five deer left behind were nodding at each other knowingly. But just then the deer out in front went quite stiff, shot up in the air, and came racing back.

"What did 'ee run away for?"

"Because I had a strange feeling, like."

"Be 'er breathing?"

"Well, I don't rightly think I heard 'er *breathing*. 'Er don't seem to have no mouth, either."

130

"Do 'er have a head?"

"I couldn't rightly tell about that, either."

"Then shall I go and see this time?"

The fourth deer went out. He was really just as scared as the rest. Even so, he went all the way up to the towel and, ever so boldly, pressed his nose right against it. Then he drew back in a hurry and came dashing back towards them like an arrow.

"Ah, 'er be soft."

"Like mud, would 'er be?"

"Naw."

"Like grass?"

"Naw."

"Like the fur on bean pods?"

"Mm—summat harder than that."

"What could 'er be, now?"

"Any rate, 'er be a living crittur."

"'Ee think so, after all?"

"Aye, 'er be *sweaty*."

"I'm thinking I'll go and have a look."

The fifth deer in his turn crept forward slowly. This one seemed to be something of a joker, for he dangled his nose right over the towel, then gave his head a great jerk as much as to say "This is very suspicious, now." The other five deer leaped about with amusement.

This encouraged the deer out in front, and he gave the towel a great lick. But then he, too, was suddenly seized with fright and came dashing back like the wind, with his mouth open and his tongue lolling out. The others were dreadfully alarmed.

"Were 'ee bitten, then? Did 'er hurt?"

But he just shivered and shivered.

"Has your tongue come loose, then?"

Still he shivered and shivered.

"Now, what be up with 'ee? Speak up, now!"

"Phew! Ah! My tongue be all numb, like!"

"What kind of taste do 'er have?"

"No taste."

"Would 'er be alive?"

"I don't rightly know. Do 'ee go and have a look now."

"Aye."

Slowly, the last deer went forward. The others all watched, nodding their heads with interest as he bent down and sniffed at it for a while. Then, quite suddenly, he picked it up in his mouth and came back with it as though there was nothing whatsoever to be afraid of anymore. The other deer bounded up and down with delight.

"Well done! Well done! Once we've got 'er, bain't nothing to be afeared of!"

"For sure, 'er be a great dried-up slug."

"Come on now, I'll sing, so do 'ee all dance around 'er."

The deer who had said this went into the middle of the group and began to sing, and the rest began to circle round and round the towel.

They ran and circled and danced, and again and again as they did so one or the other of them would dash forward like the wind and stab the towel with his antlers or trample it with his hooves. In no time, Kaju's poor towel was all muddy and holed. Then gradually the deer's circling began to slow down.

"Ah, *now* for the dumpling!"

"Ah, a boiled dumpling 'n all!"

"Ah, 'er be quite round!"

"Ah, yum yum!"

"Ah, wonderful!"

The deer split up and gathered in a ring about the horse-chestnut dumpling. Then they all ate one mouthful of it in turn, beginning with the deer who had gone up to the towel first. The sixth and last deer got a piece hardly bigger than a bean.

Then they formed a ring again and began to walk round and round and round in a circle. Kaju had been watching the deer so intently that he almost felt he himself was one of them. He was on the point of rushing out to join them, when he caught sight of his own great, clumsy hand. So he gave up the idea, and went on concentrating on breathing quietly.

Now the sun had reached the middle branches of the alder tree and was shining with a slightly yellowish light. The deer's dance grew slower and slower. They began nodding to each other busily, and soon drew themselves up in a line facing the sun, standing perfectly straight as though they were worshiping it. Kaju watched in a dream, forgetful of everything else. Suddenly, the deer at the right-hand end of the line began to sing in a high, thin voice.

Brush drawing, *Running Deer*

> See the setting sun decline,
> Blazing out behind the leaves
> That delicately shine
> Green upon the alder tree.

Kaju shut his eyes and shivered all over at the sound of the voice, which was like a crystal flute.

Now the second deer from the right suddenly leaped up and, twisting his body to and fro, ran in and out between the others, bowing his head time and time again to the sun till finally he came back to his own place, stopped quite still, and began to sing.

> Now the sun's behind its back,
> See the leafy alder tree
> Like a mirror crack
> And shatter in a million lights.

Kaju caught his breath and himself bowed low to the sun in its glory, and to the alder tree. The third deer from the right began to sing now, bowing and raising his head busily all the while.

> Homeward though the sun may go,
> Down beyond the alder tree,
> See the grass aglow,
> Dazzling white across the plain.

It was true—the pampas grass was all ablaze, like a sea of white fire.

> Long and black the shadow lies
> On the shimmering pampas grass
> Where against the skies
> Straight and tall the alder grows.

Now the fifth deer hung his head low and started singing in a voice that was hardly more than a mutter.

> See, the sun is sinking low
> In the shimmering pampas grass.
> Ants now homeward go
> Through the moss upon the plain.

Now all the deer were hanging their heads. But suddenly the sixth deer raised his head proudly and sang:

> Shy white flower, content to pass
> Your days unnoticed in the tall
> And shimmering pampas grass—
> You are dearest of them all!

Then all the deer together gave a short, sharp call like the cry of a flute, leaped up in the air, and began to dash round and round in a ring.

A cold wind came whistling from the north. The alder tree sparkled as though it really were a broken mirror. Its leaves actually seemed to tinkle as they brushed against each other, and the plumes of the pampas grass seemed to be whirling round and round with the deer.

By now Kaju had forgotten all about the difference between himself and the deer. "Hoh! Bravo, bravo!" he cried, and rushed out from behind the pampas grass.

For one moment the deer stopped stiff and straight in alarm, then the next instant they were fleeing like leaves before a gale. Their bodies bent forward in haste, breasting the waves of silver pampas grass and the shining sunset, they fled far, far into the distance, leaving the pampas grass where they had passed glittering on and on, like the wake of a boat left on a quiet lake.

Kaju smiled a rueful smile. Then he picked up his muddy, torn towel and set off walking towards the west.

And that was all, until I heard the story from the clear autumn breeze in the late sunlight that day on the mossy plain.

Gorsh the Cellist

Gorsh was the man who played the cello at the moving picture house in town. Unfortunately, he had a reputation for being none too good a player. "None too good," perhaps, was hardly the word, for if the truth be told, he was worse than any of his fellow musicians and was forever being bullied by the conductor for that reason.

One afternoon they were all sitting in a circle backstage rehearsing the Sixth Symphony, which they were soon to perform at the town's concert hall.

The trumpets were blaring for all they were worth.

The clarinets were tootling away in support.

The violins, too, were playing like fury.

Gorsh was scraping away with the rest of them, oblivious to all else, his lips pressed tight together and his eyes as big as saucers as he stared at the music in front of him.

All of a sudden the conductor clapped his hands together.

They all stopped playing instantly, and a complete hush fell over them.

"The cello was late!" shouted the conductor. "Tum-tiddy, tiddy-tee—once more from the bit that goes tum-tiddy, tiddy-tee. Right?" They all started again from a point just before where they had got to. With his face red and his forehead all sweaty, Gorsh managed somehow to get safely past the tricky bit. And he was playing the next bit with a feeling of relief when, once again, the conductor clapped his hands.

"Cello! You're off pitch! Whatever are we to do with you? You don't think I've got time to teach you the simple scale, do you?"

The others looked sorry for Gorsh and deliberately peered at their own scores or busily set about tuning their own instruments. Hastily, Gorsh tightened his strings.

"From the bar before the last place. Right!"

They all started again. Gorsh's mouth was twisted with the effort to play right. And this time they got quite a way without trouble. He was just feeling

rather pleased with himself when the conductor scowled and clapped his hands together yet again. "Oh no—not again," thought Gorsh, with a leap of his heart. But this time, luckily, it was someone else. So Gorsh deliberately peered closely at his music, as the others had done for him just now, and did his best to look engrossed in something else.

"Well then, straight on to the next bit. Right!"

But Gorsh, with a smug feeling, had no sooner started playing when the conductor gave a great stamp with his foot and started shouting.

"It won't do. You're all at sixes and sevens. This part's the heart of the whole work, and see what a hash you're making of it. Gentlemen, we've got just ten days till the performance. We're professional musicians—how could we look people in the eyes if we let some bunch of second-rate scrapers and blowers outdo us? You, Gorsh. You're one of the chief troubles. You just don't have any *expression*. No anger, no joy—no feeling at all. And you don't keep in perfect time with the other instruments, either. You always drag along behind with your shoelaces dangling. It won't do—you must pull yourself together. It's not fair to the rest to let the illustrious name of the Venus Orchestra be dragged in the mud all because of one man. Well, then—that's enough rehearsal for today. Have a rest and be in the box at six sharp."

They all bowed, then put cigarettes in their mouths and struck matches or went outside somewhere.

With his cheap, boxlike cello held in his arms, Gorsh turned to face the wall. His mouth twisted and great tears rolled down his cheeks, but he soon pulled himself together and, all by himself, began to play again from the beginning, very softly, the part they had just done.

Late that evening, Gorsh arrived home carrying an enormous black object on his back. His home was really no more than a tumbledown old millhouse standing by the river on the outskirts of the town. He lived there all alone. His mornings he spent pruning the tomatoes in the small field surrounding the mill and picking grubs off the cabbages, but in the afternoon he always went out.

Gorsh went indoors and opened the black bundle. It was, of course, the ugly great cello he had been playing earlier that evening. He lowered it gently to the floor, then suddenly took a glass and gulped down some water out of a bucket.

Then he gave a shake of his head, sat down on a chair, and began to play the piece of music they had done that day, attacking his instrument with all the ferocity of a tiger.

Turning over the pages of the score, he played a while and thought, thought a while and played, then when he got to the end he started again from the beginning, rumbling his way through the same thing over and over again.

He went on long past midnight, till in the end he hardly knew whether it was himself playing or someone else. His expression was terrible, with bright red face and eyes all bloodshot, looking as though he might collapse at any moment.

Just then, though, somebody tapped three times on the door behind him.

"Is that you, Horsh?" Gorsh called as though half-asleep. However, it was not Horsh who pushed open the door and came walking in, but a large tortoiseshell cat that he had seen around several times before.

The cat was carrying, with enormous effort it seemed, a half-ripe tomato from Gorsh's field, which he set down in front of Gorsh.

"Oh dear," he said, "I'm tired. Carrying things is a terrible job."

"Whatever? . . ." exclaimed Gorsh.

"A present for you," said the tortoiseshell cat. "Please eat it."

All the annoyance Gorsh had been damming up inside him since earlier that day came bursting out at once.

"Who told you to bring any tomato? Do you think I'd eat something brought by the likes of you in the first place? And that tomato, what's more, comes from my field. What do you think you're up to? Picking them before they turn red! I suppose it's you, then, who's been biting at the stalks of my tomatoes and scattering them all over the place? Get out of here! Damned cat!"

All this made the cat's shoulders droop and his eyes go narrow, but he forced a grin and said, "You shouldn't get so angry, sir, it's bad for your health. Why don't you play something instead? Schumann's 'Träumerei,' say. . . . I'll be your audience."

"That's enough impertinence! From a mere cat, indeed!"

Feeling furious, Gorsh spent a while thinking of the things he'd like to do to this nuisance of a cat.

"No, don't be shy, now," said the cat. "Please. You know, I can't get to sleep unless I hear you play something."

"That's enough of your cheek! Enough, I say! Enough!"

Gorsh had gone bright red and was shouting and stamping just as the conductor had done earlier that day. Suddenly, though, he changed his mind and said, "All right then, I'll play!" Ominously, he locked the door and shut all the windows, then got his cello out and turned off the light. When he did so, the light of the moon shone halfway into the room from outside.

"What d'you want me to play?"

"... 'Träumerei.' Composed by Schumann," said the cat perfectly seriously, wiping his mouth as he spoke.

"Oh. 'Träumerei,' indeed. Would this be how it goes?"

Ominously again he tore his handkerchief into strips and stuffed up both his ears tightly. Then he stormed straight into a piece called "Tiger Hunt in India."

For a while, the cat listened with bowed head, but quite suddenly he blinked his eyes rapidly and made a leap for the door. His body collided with the door, which refused to open. This threw the cat into a great state of agitation, as though he had made some horrible mistake, and sparks crackled from his eyes and forehead. Next, sparks came from his whiskers and nose too, which tickled so that for a while he looked as though he was going to sneeze, but even so, he started trotting round as though to say "I've no time for this kind of thing." Gorsh was delighted at the effect he was producing, and began to play all the harder.

"Mr. Gorsh, that's enough, thank you," said the cat. "Quite enough. I beg you to stop. I promise I'll never tell you what to do again."

"Quiet! We're just getting to the bit where they catch the tiger."

By now the cat was leaping up and down in distress, running round and round and rubbing against the walls, which gave off a green glow for a while where he had touched them. In the end, he was whirling round and round Gorsh like a merry-go-round.

Gorsh's own head began to spin a little, so he said, "All right then, I'll let you off now." And he stopped at last.

But now the cat looked quite unconcerned. "Mr. Gorsh, there's something funny about your playing tonight, isn't there?" he said.

Gorsh felt deeply aggrieved again, but he nonchalantly got out a cigarette and put it in his mouth, then took a match and said, "What about it? Are you sure there's nothing wrong with *you*? Let's have a look at your tongue."

Rather disdainfully the cat stuck out his long, pointed tongue.

"Ha-ha! Rather rough, I'm afraid," said the cellist and without warning struck the match on the cat's tongue and lit his cigarette with it. To say the cat was startled would be putting it too mildly: waving his tongue about like a wind-mill, he rushed to the door and dashed his head against it, staggered away, then went back and banged it again, staggered, went back again, banged it once more and staggered, trying desperately to find some way of escape.

For a while Gorsh watched in amusement, then he said, "I'll let you out. So mind you don't come again. Stupid!"

He opened the door, and the cat streaked off like lightning through the pampas grass. Gorsh smiled a little as he watched him go, then went to bed and slept soundly as though a load had been lifted from his mind.

The next evening, too, Gorsh came home carrying on his back the black bundle containing his cello. Then he gulped down a great deal of water and began to scrub away at his cello exactly as on the previous evening. Soon twelve o'clock came, then one, then two, and still Gorsh went on. And he was still booming away, scarcely aware of the time or even of the fact that he was playing, when he heard someone tapping on the other side of the ceiling.

"What!... Haven't you had enough yet, cat?" he shouted, whereupon a scuffling sound came from a hole in the ceiling and a gray bird came down through it. It landed on the floor, and he found it was a cuckoo.

"So now I have birds, too," said Gorsh. "What do *you* want?"

"I want to learn music," said the cuckoo quite seriously.

"Music, eh?" said Gorsh with a smile. "But all you can sing is 'cuckoo, cuckoo,' surely?"

"Yes," said the cuckoo very earnestly, "That's right. But that's very difficult, you see."

"Difficult, indeed! The only thing that's a trouble for cuckoos is having to sing such a lot. There's nothing difficult about the actual notes, is there?"

"No, actually that's just why it's so hard. For example, if I sing like this, 'cuckoo,' and then like this, 'cuckoo,' you can tell they're different just by listening, can't you?"

"There's no difference, if you ask me."

"That means you can't distinguish properly. As far as we cuckoos are con-cerned, you could sing ten thousand 'cuckoos' and they'd all be different."

"As you like. If you're so good at it, why do you have to come to me?"

"But you see, I want to learn the scale correctly."

"What could you care about the scale?"

"Oh, but one needs it if one's going abroad."

"What could you care about going abroad?"

"So—please teach me the scale. I'll sing it with you as you play."

"Oh, dear! Look. I'll play it just three times, then when I've finished you must clear off home."

Gorsh took up his cello, scraped at the strings as he tuned them, then played, "do, re, mi, fa, so, la, ti, do."

But the cuckoo fluttered his wings agitatedly.

"No, no. That's not how it should go."

"There's no pleasing you. You try it, then."

"This is how it goes." The cuckoo bent forward slightly, braced himself, and uttered a single "cuckoo."

"Well, do you call that a scale? If it is, then the ordinary scale and the sixth Symphony are all the same to you cuckoo."

"Oh no, they're quite different."

"How?"

"One of the difficult things is when you get a lot of them in succession."

"You mean like this, I suppose?" Gorsh took up his cello again and started to play in succession, "cuckoo-cuckoo, cuckoo, cuckoo."

This delighted the cuckoo so much that halfway he began to bawl "cuckoo, cuckoo, cuckoo" in time with Gorsh. On and on he went, twisting his body for all he was worth.

In time Gorsh's hand began to hurt, so he stopped.

"Here," he said, "that's about enough, isn't it?"

But the cuckoo just narrowed his eyes regretfully and went on singing for a while off until finally he went "cuckoo, cuck—cuck—cu—" and stopped.

By now Gorsh was quite angry.

"Here, bird—if you've finished, be off with you now."

"Oh, please. Won't you play it once more? Yours seems good enough, but there's something not quite right."

"What? I'm not supposed to be learning from you. Be off with you now."

"Please, just once more. Please...," said the cuckoo, bobbing his head deferentially.

"Well, then, just this once." Gorsh got his bow ready.

"But you see, I want to learn the scale correctly."

"What could you care about the scale?"

"Oh, but one needs it if one's going abroad."

"What could *you* care about going abroad?"

"Sir—please teach me the scale. I'll sing it with you as you play."

"Oh, dear! Look. I'll play it just three times, then when I've finished you must clear off home."

Gorsh took up his cello, scraped at the strings as he tuned them, then played, "do, re, mi, fa, so, la, ti, do."

But the cuckoo fluttered his wings agitatedly.

"No, no. That's not how it should go."

"There's no pleasing you. You try it, then."

"This is how it goes." The cuckoo bent forward slightly, braced himself, and emitted a single "cuckoo."

"Well! do you call that a scale? If it is, then the ordinary scale and the Sixth Symphony are all the same to you cuckoos."

"Oh no, they're quite different."

"How?"

"One of the difficult things is when you get a lot of them in succession."

"You mean like this, I suppose?" Gorsh took up his cello again and started to play in succession, "cuckoo, cuckoo, cuckoo, cuckoo."

This delighted the cuckoo so much that halfway he began to bawl "cuckoo, cuckoo, cuckoo" in time with Gorsh. On and on he went, twisting his body for all he was worth.

In time Gorsh's hand began to hurt, so he stopped.

"Here," he said, "that's about enough, isn't it?"

But the cuckoo just narrowed his eyes regretfully and went on singing for a while, till finally he went "cuckoo, cuck—cuck—cuck—cu—" and stopped.

By now Gorsh was quite angry.

"Here, bird—if you've finished, be off with you now."

"Oh, please. Won't you play it once more? Yours seems good enough, but there's something not quite right."

"What? I'm not supposed to be learning from you. Be off with you, now."

"Please, just once more. Please . . ." said the cuckoo bobbing his head deferentially.

"Well, then, just this once." Gorsh got his bow ready.

The cuckoo gave a single "cuck!" then said, "As long as possible if you don't mind." He gave another bow.

"Heaven help us," said Gorsh and with a wry smile began to play. Again the cuckoo got quite wrapped up in things and sang for all he was worth, twisting his body to and fro.

"Cuckoo, cuckoo, cuckoo."

At first Gorsh felt very irritated, but as he played on he gradually began to have an odd feeling that it was the cuckoo, somehow, who was really hitting the notes of the scale. In fact, the more he played the more he had the feeling that the cuckoo was better than he was.

"Hah! If I go on fooling around like this I shall end up by becoming a bird myself," he said, and quite abruptly stopped playing.

The cuckoo reeled as though someone had dealt him a hefty blow on the head, then just as he had done before sang, "Cuckoo, cuckoo, cuck—cuck—cuck—" and stopped.

"Why did you stop?" he said, looking at Gorsh resentfully. "If you were a cuckoo, even the least self-respecting one, you'd have gone on at the top of your voice till your throat was too sore to go on."

"Why, you cheeky. . . . Do you think I can go on fooling around like this for ever? Come on, now, get out. Look—don't you see it's nearly dawn?" He pointed to the window.

The eastern sky was turning faintly silver where black clouds were scudding across it towards the north.

"Then won't you go on until the sun rises? Just once more. It's only a little longer."

Again the cuckoo bowed his head.

"That's enough! You seem to think you can get away with anything. Stupid bird, if you don't get out I'll pluck your feathers and eat you for breakfast." He stamped hard on the floor.

This seemed to frighten the cuckoo, for suddenly he started up and flew for the window, only to bang his head violently against the glass and flop down on the floor again.

"Look at you, going into the glass. Silly idiot!" Hastily Gorsh got up to open the window, but the window never had been the kind to slide open at a touch, and he was still rattling the frame furiously when the cuckoo slammed into it and fell again.

Gorsh could see a little blood coming from the base of his beak.

"I'm going to open it for you, so wait a moment, won't you." With great difficulty he had just got the window open a couple of inches when the cuckoo got up and, staring hard at the eastern sky beyond the window as though he was determined to succeed at all costs this time, flew off with all his energy. This time of course, he hit the window even more violently than before and fell to the floor, where he remained perfectly still for a while. But when Gorsh put a hand out thinking to take him to the door and let him fly away, the bird suddenly opened his eyes and leaped out of the way. Then he made as though he was going to fly into the window again, so almost without thinking, Gorsh raised his leg and gave the window a great kick.

Two or three panes shattered with a tremendous crash and the window fell outside, frame and all. Through the gaping hole where the window had been the cuckoo flew out like an arrow. On and on he flew into the distance till finally he completely disappeared from sight. For a while Gorsh stayed looking out in disgust, then flopped down in a corner of the room and went to sleep where he was.

❧

The next night, too, Gorsh was playing his cello until past midnight. He was tired and was drinking a glass of water when again there came a tapping at the door.

Whoever came tonight, he told himself, he would take a threatening attitude from the start and drive him away before the same thing happened as with the cuckoo. As he waited with the glass in his hand, a badger cub came in. Gorsh opened the door a little wider, then stamped on the floor.

"You, badger," he shouted, "d'you know what badger soup is?" But the badger seated himself tidily on the floor with a vague kind of expression and sat thinking for a while with a puzzled look and his head tilted to one side.

"Badger soup?" said the badger in a little voice. "No."

The look on the cub's face made Gorsh want to burst out laughing, but he put on a fierce expression and went on, "Then I'll tell you. Badger soup, you see, is a badger just like you boiled up with cabbage and salt for the likes of me to eat." But the young badger looked puzzled and said, "But my father, you know, he said I was to go and study with Mr. Gorsh because he was a very nice man and not at all to be scared of."

144

At this Gorsh finally laughed out loud. "What did he tell you to study?" he said. "I'm busy, I'll have you know. And I'm sleepy, too."

The small badger stepped forward as though he had suddenly taken heart.

"You see, I'm the one who plays the side drum," he said, "and I was told to go and learn how to play in time with the cello."

"But I don't see any side drum."

"Here—look." The badger produced two sticks that were slung over his back.

"And what are you going to do with those?"

"Play 'The Happy Coachman,' please, and you'll see."

"'The Happy Coachman'? What's that—jazz or something?"

"Here's the music."

This time the badger brought from behind his back a single sheet of music. Gorsh took it from him and laughed.

"Well, this is a funny piece of music! All right! Here we go then. So you're going to play the drum, are you?" He started playing, watching the cub out of the corner of his eye to see what he would do.

But the badger started busily to beat time with his sticks on the body of the cello below the bridge. He was not at all bad at it, and as he played, Gorsh found himself beginning to enjoy things.

When they got to the end, the badger stayed thinking for a while with his head to one side. At last he seemed to reach some conclusion, for he said, "When you play this second string you get behind, don't you? Somehow it seems to throw me off the beat."

Gorsh was taken aback. It was true: ever since yesterday evening he'd had a feeling that however smartly he played that particular string there was always a pause before it sounded.

"You know, you may be right. This cello's no good," he said sadly. The badger looked sympathetic and thought again for a while.

"I wonder where it's no good. Would you mind playing it once more?"

"Of course I will." Grosh started playing. The badger beat away as before, tilting his head to one side from time to time as though listening to the cello. And by the time they had finished there was a glimmering of light again in the east.

"Look—it's getting near dawn. Thank you very much." Hastily the little badger hoisted the sticks and the music onto his back, fastened them there with a rubber band, gave two or three bows, and hurried out of the house.

For a while Gorsh sat there abstractedly, breathing in the cool air that came through the window panes he'd broken the previous night, then decided to go to sleep and get his strength back for going into town, and crawled into bed.

❧

The next night too, Gorsh was up all night playing his cello. It was near dawn, and he had begun to doze with the score still held in his hand when again he heard someone tapping. It was so faint that it was hard to be sure whether somebody had really knocked or not, but Gorsh, who was used to it by now, heard at once and said, "Come in."

Through a crack in the door there came a field mouse leading an extremely small child mouse. Hesitantly, she came towards Gorsh. As for the baby mouse, it was so small, only about as big as an eraser, that Gorsh couldn't help smiling. Peering about her as though wondering what he could be smiling at, the mouse set down a green chestnut in front of her and bowed very correctly.

"Mr. Gorsh," she said, "This child here is not well, and I'm afraid he may die. I beg you, out of the kindness of your heart, to cure him."

"How d'you expect *me* to play the doctor?" demanded Gorsh rather petulantly. The mother field mouse looked down at the floor and was silent for a while. Then she seemed to summon up her courage and said, "I know quite well that you cure all kinds of people very skillfully every day."

"I don't know what you're talking about."

"But it was thanks to you that the rabbit's grandmother got better, wasn't it, and the badger's father, and even that nasty old owl was cured, wasn't he, so in the circumstances I think it's very unkind of you to say you won't save this child."

"Wait a minute—there must be some mistake. *I've* never cured any sick owl. Though it's true I had the young badger here last night, behaving like a member of the band."

He laughed, looking down at the baby mouse in dismay.

But the mother mouse started crying.

"Ah, if the child had to get sick I only wish he'd done it sooner. To think that you were rumbling away so busily only a while ago, then as soon as he gets sick the sound stops dead, and you refuse to play any more however much I beg you. Ah, unhappy child!"

"What?" shouted Gorsh, startled. "You mean that when I play sick rabbits and owls get better? Why, I wonder?"

"You see," said the field mouse, rubbing at her eyes with a paw, "Whenever the folk around here get sick, they creep under the floor of your house to cure themselves."

"And you mean they get better?"

"Yes, it improves the circulation wonderfully. They feel so much better. Some of them are cured on the spot, others after they're back home again."

"Ah, I see. You mean that when my cello rumbles it acts as a kind of massage and cures your sicknesses for you. All right. Now I understand. I'll play for you." He squeaked at the strings a bit to tune them, then all of a sudden picked up the mouse's child between his fingers and popped him in through the hole in the cello.

"I'll go with him," said the mother mouse frantically, jumping onto the cello. "It's the same at every hospital."

"So you're going in as well, eh," said Gorsh and tried to help her in through the hole in the cello, but she could only get her face halfway in.

"Are you all right there?" she cried to the child inside as she struggled. "Did you fall properly as I always tell you you should, with your paws all four-square?"

"I'm all right. I fell nicely," came the baby mouse's voice from the bottom of the cello, so faint it could hardly be heard.

"Of course he's all right," said Gorsh. "So we don't want you crying, now."

Gorsh set the mother mouse down on the floor, then took up his bow and rumbled and scraped his way through some rhapsody or other. The mother mouse sat listening anxiously to the quality of the sound, but finally, it seemed, she could bear the suspense no longer and said, "That's enough, thank you. Please be kind enough to take him out."

"Well? Is that all?" Gorsh tipped the cello over, put his hand by the hole and waited. Almost immediately, the baby mouse appeared. Without saying anything, Gorsh set him down on the floor. The baby's eyes were shut tight and he was trembling and trembling as though he would never stop.

"How was it? How do you feel? Better?" asked the mother mouse.

The child mouse made no reply but sat with his eyes shut, trembling and trembling for a while, then quite suddenly he jumped up and started running about.

"Ah, he's better! Thank you so much, sir, thank you so much." The mother mouse went and ran about a little with her child, but soon came back to Gorb and, bowing busily over and over again, said, "Thank you so much, thank you so much," about ten times in all.

Somehow Gorb felt rather sorry for them.

"Here," he said, "do you eat bread?"

The field mouse looked shocked. "Oh, no!" she said, looking about her uneasily as she spoke. "People do say that bread is very light and airy and good to eat—it seems they make it by kneading flour—but of course we've never been near your cupboard, and we'd never dream of coming to steal it after everything you've done for us."

"No—that's not what I mean, I'm just asking if you can eat it. Yes, I see you do. Wait a moment, then I'll give some to this boy for his bad stomach."

He set the cello down on the floor, went to the cupboard, tore off a handful of bread, and put it down in front of the field mouse.

The field mouse cried and laughed and bowed as though she had gone quite silly, then with a great show of care took the bread in her mouth and went out, shooing the child in front of her.

"Dear me," said Gorb, "it's quite tiring, talking to mice." He flopped down on his bed and was soon fast asleep and snoring.

❧

It was the evening of the sixth day after this. With flushed faces the members of the Venus Orchestra, each carrying his instrument in his hand, came straggling from the stage of the town hall to the musicians' room at the back. They had just performed the Sixth Symphony with great success in the hall, the storm of applause was still continuing. The conductor, his hands thrust in his pockets, was slowly pacing about among the others as though applause meant absolutely nothing to him, but in fact he was thoroughly delighted. Some of them were putting cigarettes in their mouths, some were striking matches, and some were putting their instruments away in their cases.

The clapping was still going on in the hall. In fact, it was getting steadily louder, and was beginning to sound alarmingly as though it might get out of hand. The master of ceremonies came in with a large white rosette pinned on his chest.

"Ah, he's better! Thank you so much, sir, thank you so much." The mother mouse went and ran about a little with her child, but soon came back to Gorsh and, bowing busily over and over again, said, "Thank you so much, thank you so much," about ten times in all.

Somehow Gorsh felt rather sorry for them.

"Here," he said, "do you eat bread?"

The field mouse looked shocked. "Oh, no!" she said, looking about her uneasily as she spoke. "People do say that bread is very light and airy and good to eat—it seems they make it by kneading flour—but of course we've never been near your cupboard, and we'd never dream of coming to steal it after everything you've done for us."

"No—that's not what I mean. I'm just asking if you can eat it. Yes, I see you do. Wait a moment, then I'll give some to this boy for his bad stomach."

He set the cello down on the floor, went to the cupboard, tore off a handful of bread, and put it down in front of the field mouse.

The field mouse cried and laughed and bowed as though she had gone quite silly, then with a great show of care took the bread in her mouth and went out, shooing the child in front of her.

"Dear me," said Gorsh. "It's quite tiring talking to mice." He flopped down on his bed and was soon fast asleep and snoring.

It was the evening of the sixth day after this. With flushed faces the members of the Venus Orchestra, each carrying his instrument in his hand, came straggling from the stage of the town hall to the musicians' room at the back. They had just performed the Sixth Symphony with great success. In the hall, the storm of applause was still continuing. The conductor, his hands thrust in his pockets, was slowly pacing about among the others as though applause meant absolutely nothing to him, but in fact he was thoroughly delighted. Some of them were putting cigarettes in their mouths, some were striking matches, and some were putting their instruments away in their cases.

The clapping was still going on in the hall. In fact, it was getting steadily louder and was beginning to sound alarmingly as though it might get out of hand. The master of ceremonies came in with a large white rosette pinned on his chest.

"They're calling for an encore," he said. "Do you think you could play something short for them?"

"Afraid not," replied the conductor stiffly. "There's nothing we could do to our own satisfaction after such a major work."

"Then won't you go out and say a word to them?"

"No. Hey, Gorsh. Go and play something for them will you?"

"Me?" said Gorsh, thoroughly taken aback.

"You—yes, you," said the concertmaster suddenly, raising his head.

"Come on, now. On you go," said the conductor.

The others thrust Gorsh's cello into his hands, opened the door, and gave him a shove onto the stage. Holding the cello, beside himself with embarrassment, he appeared on the stage, whereupon everybody clapped still more loudly as though to say, "there, you see!" Some people even seemed to be cheering.

"Just how much fun do they think they can make of a fellow?" thought Gorsh. "Right—I'll show 'em. I'll play them 'Tiger Hunt in India.'"

Quite calmly, he went out into the middle of the stage. And he played "Tiger Hunt" with all the energy of an angry elephant, just as he had done the time the cat had come. But a hush fell over the audience, and they listened for all they were worth. Gorsh ploughed steadily on. The part where the cat had given off sparks of distress came and went. The part where it had thrown itself again and again against the door also came and went.

When the work finally came to an end, Gorsh gave not so much as a glance at the audience, but, taking up his cello, made a bolt for it, just as the cat had done, and took refuge in the musicians' room. But there he found the conductor and all his other colleagues sitting quite silent, gazing straight in front of them as though there had just been a fire.

No longer caring what happened, Gorsh walked briskly past them, plumped himself on a sofa at the other side of the room, and crossed his legs.

The all turned their faces in his direction and looked at him, but their expressions were earnest and they showed no sign of laughing.

"There's something funny about this evening," Gorsh thought to himself. But the conductor stood up and said, "Gorsh, you were wonderful! The music may not be much, but you kept us listening. You've improved a lot during the past week or ten days. Why, comparing it with ten days ago is like comparing a green recruit with an old campaigner. I always knew you could if you tried, Gorsh!"

The others, too, came over to him and said, "Well done!"

"You see," the conductor was saying in the background. "He can do it because he's strong; it would kill any ordinary man."

Late that night, Gorsh went back home.

First, he had a good drink of water. Then he opened the window and looking into the distant sky in the direction where he felt the cuckoo had gone, he said,

"You know, cuckoo—I'm sorry about what happened. I shouldn't have got angry like that."

The others, too, came over to him and said, "Well done!"

"You see," the conductor was saying in the background, "he can do it because he's strong. It would kill any ordinary man."

Late that night, Gorsh went back home.

First, he had a good drink of water. Then he opened the window and, looking into the distant sky in the direction where he felt the cuckoo had gone, he said, "You know, cuckoo—I'm sorry about what happened. I shouldn't have got angry like that."

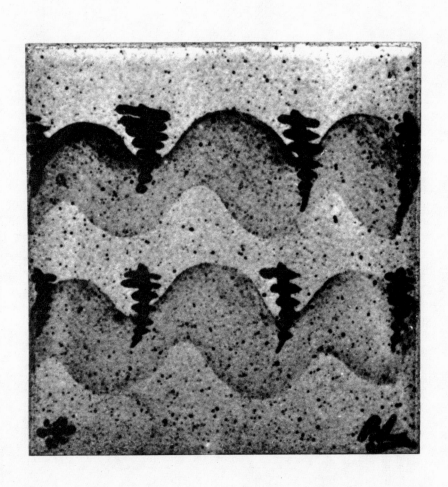

Stoneware tile, *Mountains and Pines*

The Kenju Wood

With his kimono fastened by a piece of rope and a smile on his face, Kenju would often stroll through the woods or along the paths between the fields. When he saw the green thickets in the rain, his eyes would twinkle with pleasure, and when he caught sight of a hawk soaring up and up into the blue sky he would jump for pure joy and clap his hands to tell everyone about it.

But the children made such fun of him that in time he began to pretend not to laugh. When a gust of wind came and the leaves on the beech trees shimmered in the light so that his face could not help smiling with pleasure, he would force his mouth open and take big, heavy breaths to cover it up as he stood gazing and gazing up into the boughs.

Sometimes as he laughed his silent laugh with his mouth wide open, he would rub his cheek with his finger, as though it itched. Seen from a distance, Kenju looked as though he was scratching himself by his mouth or maybe yawning, but from close, of course, you could hear he was laughing and you could tell that his lips were twitching, so the children made fun of him just the same.

If his mother had told him to, he could have drawn as many as five hundred bucketfuls of water at one time. He could have weeded the fields, too, in a single day. But his mother and father never told him to do such things.

Behind Kenju's house, there lay a stretch of open ground, as big as the average sports field, that had been left uncultivated. One year, while the mountains were still white with snow and the new grass had yet to put out buds on the plain, Kenju suddenly came running up to the other members of his family who were tilling the rice fields, and said, "Mother, buy me seven hundred cedar seedlings, will you?"

Kenju's mother stopped wielding her gleaming new hoe and stared at Kenju.

"And where are you going to plant seven hundred cedars?" she asked.

"On the open land at the back of the house."

"Kenju," said Kenju's elder brother, "you'd never get cedars to grow there. Why don't you help us a bit with the rice field instead?"

Kenju fidgeted uncomfortably and looked down at the ground.

But just then Kenju's father straightened up, wiping the sweat off his face.

"Buy them for him, buy them," he said. "Why, he's never asked us to buy a single thing for him before. Let him have them." Kenju's mother smiled as though relieved.

Full of joy, Kenju ran straight off in the direction of the house. He got an iron-headed hoe out of the barn and began turning up the turf to make holes for planting the cedars.

His elder brother, who had come after him, saw what he was doing and said, "Kenju, you have to dig deeper when you plant cedars. Wait till tomorrow. I'll go and buy the seedlings for you."

Unhappily, Kenju laid down the hoe.

The next day the sky was clear, the snow on the mountains shone pure white, and the larks chirped merrily as they soared up and up into the sky. And Kenju, grinning as though he could scarcely repress his joy, started digging holes for the seedlings just as his brother told him, beginning at the northern edge of the land. He dug them in absolutely straight rows and at absolutely regular intervals. His elder brother planted one seedling in each hole in turn.

At this point, Heiji, who owned a field to the north of the piece of open ground, came along. He had a pipe in his mouth, and his hands were tucked inside his clothes and his shoulders hunched up as though he was cold. Heiji did a little farming, but in reality he made a good part of his living in other, not so pleasant ways.

"Hey, Kenju!" he called. "You really are stupid, aren't you, to plant cedars in a place like this! In the first place, they'll shut off the sunlight from my field."

Kenju went red and looked as though he wanted to say something, but couldn't get it out and stood fidgeting helplessly.

So Kenju's elder brother, who was working a little way off said, "Good morning, Heiji." He stood up, and Heiji ambled off again, muttering to himself as he went.

Nor was it Heiji alone who poked fun at Kenju for planting cedars on that stretch of grassy land. Everybody said the same things: no cedars would grow in a place like that; there was hard clay underneath; a fool was always a fool, after all.

And they were quite right. For the first five years, the green saplings grew straight up towards the sky, but from then on their heads grew round and in both the seventh and eighth years their height stayed at around nine feet.

One morning, as Kenju was standing in front of the grove, a farmer came along to have some fun with him.

"Hey, Kenju. Aren't you going to prune those trees of yours?"

"Prune? What do you mean?"

"Pruning means cutting off all the lower branches with a hatchet."

"Then I think I'll prune them."

Kenju ran and fetched a hatchet. Then he set about mercilessly lopping off the lower branches of the cedars. But since the trees were, after all, only nine feet high, he had to stoop somewhat in order to get underneath them.

By dusk, every tree had been stripped of all its branches save for three or four at the very top. The grass below was covered with a layer of dark green branches, and the tiny wood lay bright and open.

All of a sudden it had become so empty that Kenju was upset and felt almost guilty.

Kenju's elder brother, who came back just then from working in the fields, cou'd not help smiling when he saw the wood. Then he said good-naturedly to Kenju, who was standing there looking blank, "Come on, let's gather the branches. We've got the stuff for a fine fire here. And the wood looks much better now, too."

This made Kenju feel easier at last, and together with his brother he went in under the trees and collected together all the branches that he had cut off. The grass beneath the trees was short and neat; it looked like the kind of place where you might well find two hermits playing chess.

But the next day, as Kenju was picking the worm-eaten beans out of the store in the barn, he heard a fearful clamor over in his wood. From all directions came voices giving orders, voices imitating bugles, feet stamping the ground, then suddenly a great burst of laughter that sent all the birds of the neighborhood flying up into the air. Startled, Kenju went to see what was going on.

And there, to his astonishment, he found a good fifty children on their way home from school, all drawn up in a line and marching in step between the rows of trees.

Whichever way one went, of course, the rows of trees formed an avenue. And the trees themselves, in their green costumes, looked as though they, too, were marching in lines, which delighted the children still more immeasurably. They were parading up and down between the trees with flushed faces, calling to each other as shrilly as a flock of shrikes.

In no time at all, the rows of trees had been given names—Tokyo Street, Russia Street, Western Street. . . . Kenju was delighted. Watching from behind a tree, he opened his mouth wide and laughed out loud.

From then on, the children gathered there every day. The only times they did not come were when it was raining. On those days, Kenju would stand alone outside the grove, drenched to the skin in the rain that rustled down from the soft white sky.

"On guard at the wood again, Kenju?" people would say with a smile as they went by in their straw raincoats. There were brown cones on the cedars, and from the tips of the fine green branches cold, crystal-clear drops of rain came splashing down. With his mouth wide open Kenju laughed great breaths of laughter, standing on and on, never tiring, while the steam rose from his body in the rain.

One misty morning, though, Kenju suddenly bumped into Heiji in the place where people gathered rushes for thatching. Heiji looked carefully all around, then shouted at Kenju with an unpleasant, wolflike expression.

"Kenju! Cut your trees down!"

"Why?"

"Because they shut off the light from my field."

Kenju looked down at the ground without saying anything. At the most, the shadow of the cedars did not extend more than six inches into Heiji's field. What was more, the trees actually protected it from the strong south winds.

"Cut them down! Cut them down! You won't?"

"No! I won't," said Kenju rather fearfully, lifting his head. His lips were tense as though he might burst into tears at any moment. It was the only time in his whole life that he had ever said anything in defiance of another.

But Heiji, who felt annoyed at being snubbed by someone as easygoing as Kenju, suddenly flew into a rage, and squaring his shoulders began without warning to strike Kenju across the face. He struck him heavily, again and again.

Kenju let himself be struck in silence, with one hand held against his cheek, but before long everything about him went dark and he began to stagger. At this even Heiji must have begun to feel uncomfortable, for he hastily folded his arms and stalked off into the mist.

That autumn, Kenju died of typhus. Heiji, too, had died of the same sickness only ten days before. Yet every day the children gathered in the wood just as before, quite unconcerned about such matters.

156

The next year, the railway reached the village, and a station was built a mile or so from Kenju's house. Here and there, great china factories and silk mills sprang up. In time, the fields and paddies all about were eaten up by houses. Almost before people realized it, the village had become a fullfledged town. Yet by some chance Kenju's wood was the one thing that remained untouched. The trees, moreover, were still barely ten feet high, and still the children gathered there every day. Since a primary school had been built right close by, they gradually came to feel that the wood and the stretch of turf to the south of the wood were an extension of their own playground.

By now, Kenju's father was quite white haired. And well he might be, for already it was close to twenty years since Kenju had died.

One day a young scholar, who had been born in what was then the village and was now a professor in some university in America, came to visit his old home for the first time in fifteen years. Yet look as he might, he could find no trace of the old fields and forests. Even the people of the town were mostly newcomers from other parts.

Then, one day, the professor was asked by the primary school to come and give a talk about foreign countries in the school hall. When the talk was over, the professor went out into the playground with the principal and the other teachers, then walked on in the direction of Kenju's wood.

Suddenly, the young professor stopped in surprise and adjusted his spectacles repeatedly as though he doubted what he saw. Then at last he said, almost as though to himself, "Why, this is absolutely as it used to be! Even the trees are just as they always were. If anything, they seem to have got smaller. And the childen are playing there. Why, I almost feel I might find myself and my old friends among them." Then abruptly he smiled, as though suddenly recalling where he was, and said to the principal, "Is this a part of the school playground now?"

"No. The land belongs to the house over there, but they leave it for the children to play on just as they please. So in practice it's become a kind of additional playground for the school, even though it's not really so."

"That's rather remarkable, isn't it? I wonder why it should be?"

"Ever since this place became built up everybody's been urging them to sell, but the old man, it seems, says it's the only thing he has to remember Kenju by, and that however hard up he is he will never let it go."

"Yes, yes—I remember. We used to think that Kenju was a bit wanting up

too. He was forever laughing in a breathy kind of way. He used to stand just here every day and watch us children playing. They say it was he who planted all these trees. Ah me, who's to say who is wise and who is foolish? All one can say is that fate works in wondrous ways. This will always be a beautiful park for the children. How about it—how would it be if you called it the "Kenju Wood" and kept it this way forever?"

"Now, that's a splendid idea! How happy the children would be."

And so that was how it happened.

Right in the center of the grass, in front of the children's wood, they set up an olive-colored slab of rock inscribed with the words "Kenju Wood."

Many letters and much money poured in to the school from attorneys and navy officers and people with their own small farms in lands across the sea, all of whom had once been pupils at the school.

Kenju's family cried, they were so overjoyed.

Who can tell how many thousands of people learned what true happiness was thanks to the lovely trees of the Kenju Wood, with their splendid dark green, their high scent, their cool shade in summer, and the turf with the color of moon-light that lay beneath.

And when it rained, the trees would drip great, cold, crystal-clear drops onto the turf below, and when the sun shone, they would breathe out clean, new air all about them, just as they had done when Kenju himself was there.

top. He was forever laughing in a breathy kind of way. He used to stand just here every day and watch us children playing. They say it was he who planted all these trees. Ah me, who's to say who is wise and who is foolish? All one can say is that fate works in wondrous ways. This will always be a beautiful park for the children. How about it—how would it be if you called it the "Kenju Wood" and kept it this way forever?"

"Now, that's a splendid idea! How happy the children would be."

And so that was how it happened.

Right in the center of the grass in front of the children's wood, they set up an olive-colored slab of rock inscribed with the words "Kenju Wood."

Many letters and much money poured in to the school from attorneys and army officers and people with their own small farms in lands across the seas, all of whom had once been pupils at the school.

Kenju's family cried, they were so overjoyed.

Who can tell how many thousands of people learned what true happiness was, thanks to the cedar trees of the Kenju Wood, with their splendid dark green, their fresh scent, their cool shade in summer, and the turf with the color of moonlight that lay beneath.

And when it rained, the trees would drip great, cold, crystal-clear drops onto the turf below, and when the sun shone they would breathe out clean, new air all about them, just as they had done when Kenju himself was there.

The Red Blanket

The Old Snow Woman was away, far away. With her pointed ears like a cat's and her swirling ashen hair, she was far, far away beyond the ragged, gleaming clouds over the western mountains.

Wrapped in a red blanket, his mind full of thoughts of homemade candy, a solitary child was hurrying impatiently homeward past the foot of a snow-covered hillock shaped like a great elephant's head.

"I'll make a cone of newspaper," he told himself, "and I'll puff and puff till the charcoal burns up bright and blue. Then I'll put a handful of brown sugar in the candy pan, and then a handful of crystal sugar. Then I'll add some water, and all that'll be left will be to boil it, bubble, bubble, bubble . . . "

No doubt about it, he had no thought for anything but homemade candy as he hurried on his way home.

All the while, up there in the cold, crystal-clear regions of the sky, the sun was busy stoking his dazzling white fire. The light from it shone out in all directions; some of it, falling down to earth, transformed the snow on the hushed uplands into a dazzling sheet of white icing.

Two snow wolves, with their bright red tongues lolling, were walking near the top of the hillock shaped like an elephant's head. Snow wolves are invisible to human beings, but once the wind has set them raging, they will leap up off the snow at the edge of the uplands and rush hither and thither about the sky, treading the swirling snow clouds.

"To heel! Didn't I tell you not to go too far away?" came a voice behind the snow wolves.

It was the Snow Boy, who came walking slowly with his three-cornered cap of polar bear fur set on the back of his head and his face bright and ruddy like an apple.

The snow wolves shook their heads and wheeled round, then were off again, panting, their red tongues lolling. The Snow Boy gazed up at the bright blue sky and shouted greeting to the invisible stars beyond it. The blue light pulsed down

in steady waves from the sky, and already the snow wolves were far in the distance, their red tongues darting like flames.

"To heel, I said! To heel!" cried the Snow Boy, dancing with rage till his shadow, which had lain clear and black on the snow, changed to a gleaming white light. And the wolves came darting back in a straight line with ears pricked.

Swift as the wind, the Snow Boy climbed the hill shaped like an elephant's head. The snow on the hill had been raised in lumps like seashells by the wind, and at its summit stood a great chestnut tree bearing a sprig of mistletoe with beautiful, golden, spherical fruit.

"Fetch me some!" ordered the Snow Boy as he climbed the hill. At the very first flash of his master's small white teeth, one of the wolves had bounced like a ball into the tree and was chewing at the small branch bearing the golden berries. His shadow fell far and wide over the snow as his head moved busily to and fro up in the tree. In no time, the green bark and yellow pith of the branch were ripped through, so that it fell at the Snow Boy's feet just as he reached the top of the hill.

"Thank you," said the Snow Boy. As he picked it up, his gaze swept over the landscape to the handsome town standing far away on the white and indigo plain. The river glittered, and white smoke rose from the railway station. The Snow Boy dropped his gaze to the foot of the hill. Along the narrow path through the snow that skirted it, the child in the red blanket was hurrying intently towards his home in the hills.

"That's the one who was pushing the sledge of charcoal yesterday," thought the Snow Boy. "He's bought himself some sugar and is coming back alone."

He laughed and flicked the sprig of mistletoe he held in his hand toward the child. It flew straight as a bullet and landed before the child's very nose.

The child was startled. He picked up the branch and looked about him wide-eyed. The Snow Boy laughed and cracked his whip. Then from all over the cloud-less, polished, deep blue sky, white snow began to fall like feathers from a snowy heron; it made that quiet, lovely Sunday of snow on the plain below, of amber light and brown cypress trees, more beautiful than ever. The child began to walk as fast as he could, still clutching the mistletoe in his hand.

But then, just as this harmless snow stopped falling, the sun seemed to move farther away in the sky, to the resting place where he replenishes his dazzling white fires. A slight breeze sprang up from the northwest. The sky had turned bitterly cold. From far off to the east, in the direction of the sea, there came a tiny sound as though something had slipped in the sky's mechanism, and small shapes seemed to pass rapidly across the face of the sun, which was a great white mirror by now.

The Snow Boy tucked his leather whip under his arm, folded his arms tightly, pressed his lips together, and gazed steadily in the direction from which the wind was blowing. The wolves stretched their necks out straight and gazed intently in the same direction.

The wind grew steadily stronger, and the snow at their feet rustled steadily as it streamed away behind them. Soon, what looked like a column of white smoke was to be seen standing on the peaks of the distant mountain range, and all at once the west was dark and gray all over.

The Snow Boy's eyes blazed fiercely. The sky turned white, the wind seemed to be tearing everything apart; the snowflakes came, dry and powdery. Then the air was full of ashen snow, though whether it was really snow or cloud was hard to tell.

All at once, the ridges of the hills began to give out a sound, a kind of creaking and swishing. Horizon and town disappeared beyond the dark vapor, leaving only the white shape of the Snow Boy dimly visible as he stood erect in the storm.

Then, from amidst the rending and the howling of the wind, there came another, stranger voice.

"Whew! Why do you tarry? Come, snow! Whew! Whew! Come, snow! Come, blow! Why do you tarry? Is there not work to do? Wheew! Wheew! See, I bring three with me from yonder! Come, snow! Whew!"

The Snow Boy leaped up as though electrified: the Old Snow Woman had arrived.

Crack! went the Snow Boy's whip, and the snow wolves bounded forward. His face grew pale, his lips tightened together, his hat flew away in the wind.

"Whew! Whew! To work, to work! No idling! Whew! Whew! To work! To work! Whew!"

The Old Snow Woman's cold white locks swirled round and round in the snow and wind; her pointed ears and glittering gold eyes were visible among the scurrying black clouds. Already the three snow boys she had brought with her from the western plain were rushing to and fro unceasingly, with deathly pale faces and lips clamped tight together, too busy even to exchange greetings with one another. Soon hills, driving snow and sky were quite undistinguishable; the only sounds were the shrieks of the Old Snow Woman as she went to and fro, the cracking of the snow boys' whips, and the panting of the nine snow wolves as they rushed about in the newly fallen snow.

And then, in the midst of it all, the Snow Boy heard the voice of the child, crying. An odd light gleamed in his eyes. He stopped for a moment and thought.

Then, cracking his whip fiercely, he rushed off to find the child.

But he must have mistaken the direction, for he collided with a black pine-clad hill far off to the south. So he tucked his whip under his arm and pricked up his ears.

"Whew! Whew!" came the Old Snow Woman's voice. "I'll have no idling! Come, snow! Snow! Come, snow! Whew! Whew, whew! Whew!"

Once more, from amidst the raging of wind and snow, he caught the thin, transparent sound of a child crying. Straight as a die, the Snow Boy ran in its direction, the Old Snow Woman's dishevelled locks, wrapping themselves unpleasantly round his face as he went. And there, on the pass over the hill, he found the child in the red blanket, alone in the raging storm, where he had toppled over with his feet stuck firmly in the snow. He was crying and thrusting one hand into the snow in a effort to get himself up.

"Lie back and pull the blanket over you!" shouted the Snow Boy as he ran. "Lie back and pull the blanket over you. Whew!"

But the child heard only the voice of the wind and saw nothing.

"Fall over on your back," cried the Snow Boy, running back again. "Whew! You mustn't move it will soon be over, so lie back with the blanket over you!"

But the child still struggled to get up.

"Lie down!" cried the Snow Boy, rushing past again. "Whew! be quiet and fall down on your back! It's not so cold today, you won't freeze."

Again the child tried to get up, weeping all the while, his mouth twisted and trembling with fear.

"Lie down! Oh, it's no use! And the Snow Boy deliberately gave the child a great buffeting, so that he fell over.

"Whew! The Old Snow Woman had come up. "Harder to work! No idling, now! On, on! Whew!" He could see the purple slit of her mouth and her pointed teeth looming through the storm. "Oho! Here's a funny child! That's right! We'll have him. Why at this time of year we've a right to one or two at the very least."

"Of course we have," said the Snow Boy. "Here, that'll finish you!" And he deliberately gave the child another buffeting. But softly he whispered to him. "I mustn't move, do you hear?"

The snow wolves were still rushing about madly, their black paws darting in

And then, in the midst of it all, the Snow Boy heard the voice of the child, crying. An odd light gleamed in his eyes. He stopped for a moment and thought. Then, cracking his whip fiercely, he rushed off to find the child.

But he must have mistaken the direction, for he collided with a black, pine-clad hill far off to the south. So he tucked his whip under his arm and pricked up his ears.

"Whew! Whew!" came the Old Snow Woman's voice. "I'll have no idling! Come, snow! Snow! Come, whew! Whew! Whew, whew! Whew!"

Once more, from amidst the raging of wind and snow, he caught the thin, transparent sound of a child crying. Straight as a die, the Snow Boy ran in its direction, the Old Snow Woman's dishevelled locks wrapping themselves unpleasantly round his face as he went. And there, on the pass over the hills, he found the child in the red blanket, alone in the raging storm where he had toppled over with his feet stuck firmly in the snow. He was crying and thrusting one hand into the snow in a effort to get himself up.

"Lie back and pull the blanket over you!" shouted the Snow Boy as he ran. "Lie back and pull the blanket over you. Whew!"

But the child heard only the voice of the wind and saw nothing.

"Fall over on your back," cried the Snow Boy, running back again. "Whew! You mustn't move. It will soon be over, so lie back with the blanket over you!"

But the child still struggled to get up.

"Fall down!" cried the Snow Boy, rushing past again. "Whew! Be quiet and fall down on your back! It's not so cold today, you won't freeze."

Again the child tried to get up, weeping all the while, his mouth twisted and trembling with fear.

"Lie down! Oh, it's no use!" And the Snow Boy deliberately gave the child a great buffeting, so that he fell over.

"Whew! The Old Snow Woman had come up. "Harder to work! No idling, now! On, on! Whew!" He could see the purple slit of her mouth and her pointed teeth looming through the storm. "Ohoh! Here's a funny child! That's right! We'll have him. Why at this time of year we've a right to one or two at the very least."

"Of course we have," said the Snow Boy. "Here, that'll finish you!" And he deliberately gave the child another buffeting. But softly he whispered to him, "Lie still. You mustn't move, do you hear?"

The snow wolves were still rushing about madly, their black paws darting in and out of sight amidst the whirling snow. "Well done! That's right!" cried the Old Snow Woman as she flew off again. "Come, snow! I'll have no idling. Whew!" The child tried again to get up. Laughing, the Snow Boy gave him another great buffeting. By now everything was dim and murky. It was not yet three in the afternoon, but it was as though the sun had already set. The child's strength had given out, and he did not try to get up any more. Laughing, the Snow Boy stretched out a hand and pulled the red blanket right over him.

"Now go to sleep. I'll cover you with many quilts, so you'll not freeze. Dream now of homemade candy till the morning."

Over and over again he repeated the words as he piled layer after layer of snow on the child. Soon the red blanket had disappeared, and the snow above it was smooth and even all over.

"That child still has the mistletoe I gave him," muttered the Snow Boy to himself, looking tearful for a moment.

"To work, to work!" came the Old Snow Woman's voice through the wind from afar. "No rest for us until two in the morning. No rest for us today! Come, snow! Whew! Whew-whew! Whew!"

At last, amidst wind and snow and ragged gray clouds, the sun really did set. All through the night, the snow fell and fell and fell. Then, when dawn was near, the Old Snow Woman rushed one last time straight through from south to north.

"Come, take your rest," she cried. "I must away to the sea again. You need not follow me. Rest your fill and prepare for our next meeting. Ah, how well it went! A good day indeed!"

Her eyes shone in the darkness with a strange blue light as she rushed off to the east with her rough, dry hair swirling and her mouth chattering.

Plain and hills seemed to relax, and the snow shone with a bluish white light. The sky had cleared, and starry constellations were twinkling all over the rich blue vault of heaven.

The snow boys collected their wolves and greeted each other for the first time.

"Terrific today, wasn't it?"

"Mm."

"Wonder when we shall meet again?"

"I wonder. But not more than twice again this year, I expect."

"I'm longing for us all to go home north together."

"Mm."

"A child died a while ago, didn't he?"

"It's all right. He's only asleep. Tomorrow I'll leave a mark there to show where he is."

"We'd better go. Have to be back beyond the hills by dawn."

"Goodbye, then."

"Goodbye."

The three Snow Boy's wolves with their nine wolves set off homeward to the year. Before long, the eastern sky began to shine like a yellow rose, then gleamed amber, and finally flared up all gold. Everywhere, hills and plain alike, was full of new snow.

The Snow Boy's wolves were strung limp and exhausted. The Snow Boy, too, sat down on the snow, and laughed. His cheeks were like apples and his breath had the fragrance of lilies.

The gleaming sun rose in all his glory, with a bluish tinge today that made him more splendid than ever. The new hole would flood pink with sunlight. The snow wolves got up and opened wide their mouths, from which blue flames flicked.

"Come, all of you, follow me," said the Snow Boy. "Dawn has broken, we must awaken the child."

He ran to where the child was buried beneath the snow.

"Here, scratch away the snow, just here," he ordered.

With their back legs, the snow wolves kicked up the snow, which the breeze scattered at once like smoke.

A figure wearing furs, with snowshoes on its feet, was hurrying from the direction of the village.

"That will do!" shouted the Snow Boy, seeing the edge of the child's red blanket peep out from under the snow.

"Your father is coming!" he cried, racing up the hillside in a column of powdery snow. "You must wake up now!"

The child seemed to stir a little. And the figure in furs came running for all it was worth.

"A child died a while ago, didn't he?"

"It's all right. He's only asleep. Tomorrow I'll leave a mark there to show where he is."

"We'd better go. Have to be back beyond the hills by dawn."

"Goodbye, then."

"Goodbye."

The three snow boys with their nine wolves set off homewards to the west. Before long, the eastern sky began to shine like a yellow rose, then gleamed amber, and finally flared up all gold. Everywhere, hills and plain alike, was full of new snow.

The Snow Boy's wolves were sitting limp and exhausted. The Snow Boy, too, sat down on the snow and laughed. His cheeks were like apples and his breath had the fragrance of lilies.

The gleaming sun rose in all his glory, with a bluish tinge today that made him more splendid than ever. The whole world flooded pink with sunlight. The snow wolves got up and opened wide their mouths, from which blue flames flickered.

"Come, all of you, follow me," said the Snow Boy. "Dawn has broken, we must awaken the child."

He ran to where the child was buried beneath the snow.

"Here, scratch away the snow just here," he ordered.

With their back legs, the snow wolves kicked up the snow, which the breeze scattered at once like smoke.

A figure wearing furs, with snowshoes on its feet, was hurrying from the direction of the village.

"That will do!" shouted the Snow Boy, seeing the edge of the child's red blanket peeping out from under the snow.

"Your father is coming," he cried, racing up the hillock in a column of powdery snow. "You must wake up now!"

The child seemed to stir a little. And the figure in furs came running for all it was worth.

164